Publisher:
Wildside Press, LLC

Distributor:
Curtis Circulation

Editor:
John Gregory Betancourt

Associate Editors:
Darrell Schweitzer
Sean Wallace

Assistant Editor:
P.D. Cacek

Copyright © 2007
by Wildside Press, LLC.
All rights reserved.

Adventure Tales is published
four times per year by Wildside Press LLC, 9710 Traville
Gateway Dr. #234, Rockville,
MD 20850. Postmaster & others:
send change of address and
other subscription matters to
Wildside Press, 9710 Traville
Gateway Dr. #234, Rockville,
MD 20850. Single copies:
$7.95 (magazine edition) or
$18.95 (book paper edition),
postage paid in the U.S.A. Add
$2.00 per copy for shipping
elsewhere. Subscriptions: four
issues for $19.95 in the U.S.A.
and its possessions, $29.95
in Canada, and $39.95 else-
where. All payments must be
in U.S. funds and drawn on a
U.S. financial institution. If you
wish to use PayPal to pay for
your subscription, email your
payment to: wildside@sff.net.

Tell us what you think!
Visit the official *Adventure
Tales* message board at:

www.wildsidepress.com

Wildside Press
9710 Traville Gateway Dr.
#234
Rockville, MD 20850
www.wildsidepress.com

We invite letters of comment
(via email or regular mail),
and we assume all letters
received are intended for
publication (unless marked
"Do Not Publish") and be-
come the property of Wildside Press.

CONTENTS

SPRING 2007   **Vol. 1, No. 4**

Features

THE BLOTTER, by the Editor 5
About this special "Weird Tales Authors" issue of Adventure Tales!

ADVENTURE THRILLS 20

THE MORGUE 93
Letters from our readers

Fiction

THE MONKEY GOD, by Seabury Quinn 8
A gold monkey with ruby eyes . . . and murder!

DOUBLE-SHUFFLE, by Edwin Baird 22
A fake tramp and a fake gentleman meet with unexpected results!

EVERY MAN A KING, by E. Hoffmann Price 28
Samarkand, the jewel of the Jagatai Empire, was now the prize of the Kipchak Horde!

BLIND MAN'S BLUFF, by Edwin Baird 45
There be many kinds of critics . . .

THE MAD DETECTIVE, by John D. Swain 58
"That's the way with cats in a strange place . . ."

SON OF THE WHITE WOLF, by Robert E. Howard 78
A thrill-packed novelet of Eastern intrigue!

Verse

ADVENTURE, by Clark Ashton Smith 21
ASTROPHOBOS, by H.P. Lovecraft 77
ALWAYS COMES EVENING, by Robert E. Howard 92

Artwork

Vincent di Fate 19
Thomas Floyd 3, 5, 63

WILDSIDE PULP CLASSICS: PULP FACSIMILE SERIES

Series editor: John Gregory Betancourt

#1: *Spicy Mystery Stories* (August 1935)

Includes Robert Leslie Bellem, Atwater Culpepper, Ellery Watson Calder, Carl Moore, E. Hoffman Price, Arthur Wallace, and more.

#2: *Ghost Stories* (June 1931)

Stories by Conrad Richter (author of The Light in the Forest*) and E. & H. Heron featuring psychic detective, Flaxman Low.*

#3: *Spicy Mystery Stories* (February 1937)

Features Robert Leslie Bellem, Lew Merrill (Victor Rousseau) Hugh Speer, Justin Case (Hugh B. Cave), & many others!

#4: *Strange Tales #7* (January 1933)

Features Hugh B. Cave's classic "Murgunstrumm," as well as stories by Robert E. Howard, Henry S. Whitehead, and many more.

#5: *The Black Mask #2* (May 1920)

2nd issue of classic mystery mag, where hardboiled fiction was born!

#6: *Tales of Magic and Mystery* (February 1928)

Legendary rare early fantasy magazine!

#7: *The Phantom Detective #1* (February 1933)

The premiere issue of the detective-hero pulp!

#8: *Submarine Stories* (March 1930)

Rare pulp magazine, stories and articles about (what else?) subs!

#9: *Sinister Stories #1* (Feb 1940)

The first issue of this "weird menace" pulp!

#10: *The Thrill Book* (Sept. 1, 1919)

The facsimile reprint from this legendary rare pulp magazine!

#11: *The Spider* (March 1940)

Includes the "Spider" novel Slaves of the Laughing Death!

#12: *Spicy Adventure Stories* (Dec. 1939)

As I reported in the second issue of *Adventure Tales*, Rich Harvey's annual pulp convention, PulpAdventurecon, is my favorite convention. (I don't get out much, but I make a point of attending this one every year.) The one-day event is primarily a dealers' room (this year it overflowed into two rooms) where attendees wander around, shopping for pulp magazines, books, and other vintage collectibles while chatting. Wildside Press usually has a dealer's table, and this year I brought my older son, Ian (age 12). My wife predicted that he would be bored, but she was 100% wrong—he loved every aspect of the show. He decided to collect memorabilia featuring The Shadow, and although the original pulp magazines were out of his price range, he managed to pick up two posters, a bunch of toys from the Alec Baldwin movie, and several sets of Old Time Radio records with adventures of The Shadow (Orson Welles is his favorite Shadow), Mandrake the Magician, and several others.

The men at the next table *did* give Ian quite a few bargains. They were selling off a large collection of Shadow, Phantom, and other pulp hero merchandise which their father had accumulated. But that only fed my son's sense of excitement. Now that he's thoroughly hooked, I don't think Ian will miss another PulpAdventurecon, either.

Even though Rich Harvey reported a slight dip in attendance, I think con-goers are getting younger rather than older. I saw quite a few fans in their 20s and 30s. It bodes well for the future.

For info on PulpAdventurecon, visit Rich Harvey's web site, <www.boldventurepress.com>.

We have another great theme issue this time: stories from authors who appeared in the classic *Weird Tales* magazine (but *not* stories from *Weird Tales*)!

Our lineup this time starts with Seabury Quinn. Quinn was the most prolific author in the history of *Weird Tales*, famous for his Jules de Grandin psychic detective yarns as well as many stand-alones. But he also wrote prolifically in other genres. Here we have a mystery with more than a few *weird* overtones.

Edwin Baird is represented with two stories. Not only was Baird a Chicago writer, but the very first *editor* of WT. He was the one who introduced the world to weird fiction and poetry from H.P. Lovecraft, Robert E. Howard, Clark Ashton Smith, Seabury Quinn, and hundreds of others.

E. Hoffmann Price claimed the distinction of being the only person who met both H.P. Lovecraft and Robert E. Howard . . . and was an accomplished pulp writer on his own for many decades. His story, "Every Man a King," comes from one of the "spicy" pulps, *Speed Adventure*, (as Spicy Adventure was renamed late in its life).

John D. Swain's "The Mad Detective" is one of his non-fantasies, in this case a gripping mystery.

And last but not least, here is Robert E. Howard's thrill-packed novelet of Eastern intrigue, "Son of the White Wolf." Enjoy!

— *John Gregory Betancourt*

Öwlswick Press

THE ADVENTURES OF DOCTOR ESZTERHAZY by **Avram Davidson**, with full-color dust jacket by **George Barr**, interior drawings by **Todd Cameron Hamilton**, and a foreword by **Gene Wolfe**.

Analog Science Fiction & Fact wrote: "Between 1974 and 1986, Avram Davidson published a number of stories of such astonishing skill, erudition, wit, and quirkiness that major markets such as *The New Yorker* and *Playboy* wouldn't touch them with a ten-foot Bulgarian. Set on the cusp between the nineteenth and the twentieth centuries in Scythia-Pannonia-Transbalkania, the fourth largest empire in Europe (the Turks were fifth) and a literal neighbor of the comic-opera realms of Graustark and Ruritania, flavored with Gilbert & Sullivan, Twain, Chesterton, and Conan Doyle (et only Davidson knows the cetera), they starred Engelbert Eszterhazy as a gentleman in search of learning wherever he might find it, unfazed by the strangest of events, cleverly combining the data that came his way to solve mysteries and ease the lots of the polyglot peoples of the empire. . . . Buy it."

In *Newsday*, Gregory Feeley wrote: "The stories are mannered, witty, and filled with the ornate archaisms of Davidson's mature style. . . . Davidson is the peer of John Collier and Lord Dunsany, and *The Adventures of Doctor Eszterhazy* is one of his finest books."

Tom Whitmore, in *Locus, the Newspaper of the Science Fiction Field*, wrote: "But what about these stories, I hear you ask. What are they about, and why should I read them? They are about Engelbert Eszterhazy, possessor of six doctorates; they are about the empire of Scythia-Pannonia-Transbalkania and its tribulations; they are about wonder, marvel, and the unexpected.

"They are Victorian tales, with a Victorian pace, with the richness of language that makes the best Victoriana so marvelous, and with modern allusions and understanding lurking just beneath the surface; to try to summarize them individually is to wreak havoc on their integrity. There are wonders here for those who know a little, and marvels for those who know a lot, about literature, history, botany, or any other subject.

"But you should read these stories because they are fun. They amuse, instruct, alert, puzzle, and challenge in the way that only great stories can. The publisher's conceit of having each story identified by an icon rather than a running title is totally appropriate. . . . A masterful performance from both author and publisher!"

Avram Davidson wrote *The Phoenix and the Mirror, Peregrine: Primus, Peregrine: Secundus,* and *Vergil in Averno*, along with many other classics of erudite, witty fantasy.

Hardcover, 386 pages: $24.50 postpaid from Owlswick Press, 121 Crooked Lane, King of Prussia PA 19406-2570

NEW FROM WILDSIDE PRESS!

The House of Skulls, by H. Bedford Jones
Trade paper: $19.95 Hardcover: $39.95

This new collection from the pen of H. Bedford-Jones presents five of his most exciting works from the pulp magazines of the early 20th Century, four novelets and one short story. Included are "The House of Skulls," "Written in Red," "Yellow Intrigue," "Down the Coast of Barbary," and "Skulls." Sure to please not only afficianados of pulp fiction but readers looking for some of the best adventure writing around, The House of Skulls and Other Tales from the Pulps is the latest addition to the Wildside Pulp Classics line!

Slave of Mystery, by Johnston McCulley
Trade paper: $19.95 Hardcover: $39.95

This volume presents 5 novellas by Johnston McCulley, creator of Zorro. Originally published under the pseudonym "Harrington Strong" in *Detective Story Magazine*, these mysteries showcase McCulley's lifelong devotion to the mystery field with meticulously plotted and brightly characterized stories that still hold the interest of modern readers. Presented here are "The Great Green Ring," "The Only Way," "Run to Ground," "The Obvious Clue," and "Slave of Mystery."

The Golden Dolphin, by J. Allan Dunn
Trade paper: $19.95 Hardcover: $35.00

J. Allan Dunn — one of the most popular writers for the pulps — wrote voluminously on every subject imaginable. Here are three of his swashbuckling tales of pirates, full of colorful action and daring escapades! *The Golden Dolphin*, a complete novel, tells the story of an expedition to find out what happened to a ship lost in the South Seas. "The Marooner" is the story of Long Tom Pugh, infamous buccaneer in the Caribbean, and his ship, the Scourge. "Forced Luck" tells of Barthelemy "Bart" Portuguese, superstitious freebooter, who believed a gold amulet sealed his success.

THE MONKEY GOD

by SEABURY QUINN

Professor Harvey Forrester was having a beastly time. He had confided as much to himself more than once in the past twenty-four hours, and each passing minute confirmed the truth of it.

The Professor did not dance, and the younger members of the company fox-trotted from breakfast to luncheon, from luncheon to dinner and from dinner to bedtime. The Professor did not care for music, except classical compositions or the simple folk songs of primitive peoples, and the Milsted house was filled with the cacophonies of jazz from radio and phonograph all day and three-quarters of the night. The Professor despised bridge as a moronic substitute for intelligent conversation, and the older members of the company played for a cent a point from dinner till midnight with the avidity of professional gamblers.

The Professor was having a beastly time.

But old Horatio Milsted, in honor of whose son the house party was given, possessed one of the finest collections of oriental curios in the country, wherefore Forrester had accepted the invitation tendered him and Rosalie Osterhaut, his ward; for he greatly desired to examine a certain statuette of Hanuman, the Monkey God, which was the supreme jewel in the collection that Milsted had inherited from a sea-roving (and none too scrupulous) grandsire.

Two days—forty-eight interminable hours of fox trotting, syncopated music and card-ruffling—the Professor had endured, and as yet had not caught sight of the little monkey god's effigy. Each time he broached the subject to Milsted his host put him off with some excuse. The house party would break up the following morning, and meantime the Professor cooled his back against the wall of the Milsted drawing room while his anger rose hot and seething within him.

"Oh, Professor Forrester," whispered Arabella Milsted, the host's unmarried sister, in the irritatingly high, thin voice possessed by so many short, fat women, "you look so romantically aloof standing there all by yourself. Tell me, don't you ever unbend, even for a teeny, tinsy moment?" She looked archly at him above the serrated edge of her black fan and simpered with bovine coquettishness.

"Do you know," she went on in a more confidential whisper, her little, pale-blue eyes growing circular with sudden seriousness, "I have a presentiment—a premonition—that something *terrible* is going to happen?"

"Umpf?" growled Forrester noncommittally, gazing first at the obese damsel, then across the crowded dance floor in an effort to descry an exit. "Umpf!"

"Yes —" Miss Milsted, who would never again see forty, but dressed in a manner becoming to twenty, and talked chiefly in Italics, replied—"oh, *yes;* I'm *very* psychic, you know. Poor dear Mamma used to say —"

Poor dear Mamma's profound observations will never be known to posterity, for at that moment Horatio Milsted, looking anything but the urbane host, strode into the drawing room and commanded sharply, "Shut off that infernal music!"

"Hear, hear!" murmured the Professor under his breath.

Young Carmody, a vapid-faced youth in too-fashionably cut dinner clothes, who stood nearest the radio, turned the rheostat, and the lively dance tune expired with a dismal squawk.

"Someone has been tampering with my collection," Milsted announced in a hard, metallic voice. "Some infernal thief has stolen a priceless relic—the statue of Hanuman. Now, I don't make any accusations; but I want that curio back. I think I know the thief, and while I'd be justified in turning him over to the police, I'll give him a chance to return my property without a scandal—if he will. The museum is just beyond the library. I want everyone here—*everyone*—to step into the library, then go, one at a time, into the museum. There's only one door, and the windows are barred, so the thief can't get away. Each of you will be allowed thirty seconds—by himself—in the museum. There'll be a handkerchief on the table, and if I don't find the statuette under that handkerchief when the last of you has passed through the museum, why —" he swept the company with another frigid stare—"I shall have to ask you all to wait while I send for the sheriff. Is that clear?"

A wondering, frightened murmur of assent ran round the brightly lighted room, and the host turned on his heel as he shot out, "This way, if you please."

Rosalie, the Professor's ward, glanced backward at her guardian as she accompanied her dancing partner and two other couples into the library, and the look in her wide, topaz eyes was a troubled one. She had lived with the Professor nearly a year, now, and knew him as only a woman can know the man she idolizes. The straight-backed little scientist was the soul of honor and propriety, but so immersed in his beloved study of anthropology that theft or murder would scarcely deter him from the acquisition of a relic of scientific value. "What if he should—" she shook her narrow shoulders as one who puts away an unpleasant thought, and stepped across the library threshold.

"I *know* something terrible will happen," Miss Milsted wailed softly in the Professor's ear.

"Nonsense, Madam; control yourself!" Forrester replied sharply, his narrow nostrils quivering with excitement.

The north wind, sweeping furiously across the rolling Maryland hills, hurled a barrage of sleet and snow against the windows, a man coughed with the abrupt sharpness of nervousness, and a woman tittered with embarrassment. The logs in the hall fireplace snapped and crackled; otherwise the house was as silent as a Quaker meeting before the Spirit moves. Two minutes dragged slowly by while the party in the drawing room watched the library door with bated breath. What drama was being enacted behind those unresponsive panels?

"Oh, I *know*—" the Milsted person began her dismal prophecy once more, then checked her speech with a little squeak like that of an unsuspecting mouse suddenly snared in a trap. Dying with a short flare, like a shred of dried grass touched with a match, the electric lights winked out, and, save for the reflection of the blazing logs in the hall fireplace, the house was hooded in darkness.

"Oh, I *knew* it—" Miss Milsted asserted, but Professor Forrester strode impatiently across the polished floor toward the closed door of the library.

"Control yourself, Madam," he snapped. "The wires have been short-circuited by the storm. Here, somebody, bring some candles!" It was characteristic of him that he should assume command in the emergency. The man who had braved sandstorms in the Sahara, glaciers in the Himalayas and natives of Somaliland while tracing the footprints of early civilizations was not to be daunted by imperfect electric power systems. "Fetch some candles," he repeated sharply; "we can't—"

Voices rose in angry discord behind the library door. A man's shout, a woman's scream, Milsted's half-uttered curse mingled in sudden, sharp babel, then *bang!* the wicked, whip-like snap of a pistol shot punctuated the hubbub.

The Professor was first to reach the library. He darted through the door, swinging it shut behind him, stilled the renewed voices with a single, sharp command, and struck a match, kneeling over a long, inert object stretched before the grate of glowing coke beneath the mantelpiece.

"Oh, I *know* something terrible is going to happen! I know it—" Miss Milsted screamed, clawing futilely at the coat-sleeve of the nearest man.

"Madam, be still!" the Professor's voice, dry and sharp with suppressed excitement, cut through the gloom as he re-entered the drawing room. "Be quiet; nothing terrible is going to happen. It's already happened. Mr. Milsted is dead."

"Dead!" the dreadful word flew from lip to lip about the circle of frightened guests. And, as if the tragic announcement were the cue to a theatrical electrician, the dimmed lights of the big country house suddenly sprang into brightness once more, shedding their sharp, yellow rays on the group of pale, terrified faces and bringing the rouge on lips and cheeks into ghastly prominence as frightened women turned hysterically to equally frightened men for comfort and protection.

"How—" began young Carmody, but the Professor cut him short.

"Call the nearest post of state troopers," he ordered curtly. "Then get in touch with the sheriff and the county coroner. Everyone stay where he is, please; the authorities will tell us when we may leave.

"Now"—Forrester closed the door against the chattering throng in the drawing room and faced the six people in the library—"just what happened?"

"We had just come in, Uncle Harvey," Rosalie answered, speaking with slow care, for in times of excitement her English, still only a half-familiar tongue, completely deserted her; "we had just come in here, and Mr. Milsted was deciding which one of us should go into the museum first, when the lights

went out. Somehow, just at the same time, that window there"—she pointed to a casement between two ceiling-high bookcases—"blew open, and, it seemed to me, I saw a head at the opening. I'm not sure about that, though. Mr. Carpenter here started across the room to close the window, and I think someone else did, too, though I don't know who it was, and Mr. Milsted began to swear and ran toward me, then there was a flash and a report, and—"

"And he shot himself," young Mr. Carpenter supplied, interrupting the girl's story. "I don't know why he did it, but we all saw the flash and heard him cry out with a sort of choke, and saw him fall. There was light enough from the fire for us to see that much."

"But it looked to me as though he were shooting toward the window, not at himself," Rosalie protested. "I'm sure the flash was directed away from him."

"Then how do you account for—that?" Carpenter asked almost roughly, pointing dramatically to the figure lying face downward on the handsome Persian rug.

Mr. Milsted lay prone as he had fallen, one arm oddly twisted beneath him, the other extended full length beyond his head, the stock of a German Army automatic grasped convulsively in his hand. His right cheek rested against the nap of the rug, and the Professor, bending down to look into his face, observed a small, round hole, about the caliber of a lead pencil, some two inches or so above the eyebrows and almost in the center of the forehead. The rim of the wound was a little discolored, as though from a bruise, and the center was slightly depressed, forming a shallow cup or crater, while a mass of thick, clotted matter, grayish white mixed with blood, showed within the tiny, deadly circle. One or two drops of blood—no more—had trickled from the wound and lay upon the carpet.

"Um?" Forrester rose slowly from his contemplation and pinched his narrow chin between the thumb and forefinger of his right hand. "How do you account for it? That's the question." Thrusting his hand into his jacket pocket, he drew out a short-stemmed briar pipe, stuffed it to overflowing with long cut tobacco and began puffing furiously. "I don't think we'll accomplish much huddled in here," he suggested. "Suppose you join the others. The officers should be here any moment, now."

As the door closed behind the others, Professor Forrester wheeled and stepped quickly into the museum. It was a small, square room entered by a single door of heavy, iron-bound oak, and lighted by a single small, heavily barred window. About its sides were ranged the tall glass-fronted specimen cases, all strongly fastened with Yale locks, while a small, compact safe and two tall, sheet-steel cabinets stood against the wall directly beneath the window. In the center, under the ceiling electrolier, was a table of polished mahogany on which lay a handkerchief covering two small objects. The Professor lifted the cloth, disclosing a small brass inkwell and stamp box.

"Milsted certainly intended giving the guilty man every chance," he commented softly to himself. "No one coming in here could say whether the handkerchief had covered two or three things before, and the fact that the cloth was already resting on two other things would partially disguise the fact that the idol had been returned. Yes, he was pretty decent about it, poor chap."

Replacing the square linen, he stared speculatively about the room. "Now, let's see," he murmured. "The Hanuman statue couldn't have been much bigger than this inkwell or stamp box, smaller, perhaps. Anyone could have carried it easily in his pocket. H'm; very interesting."

Strolling over to the safe, he bent forward and examined it, even testing its lock tentatively, first taking the precaution to cover the knob with his handkerchief, lest his fingerprints show on the polished metal. The lock was fastened, and he next turned his attention to the upright metal cabinets. They were nearly six feet high by eighteen inches wide and about two feet deep. One was filled with a miscellaneous assortment of papers, old letters and kindred junk, while the other was empty, even its shelves having been removed, leaving a space available for storage about as large as the interior of an upended mummy case.

Again the Professor stooped, examining the cabinet's interior carefully. "Umpf," he inquired of the empty room, "what's this?" On the smoothly painted floor of the case were four crescent-shaped ridges of sand and fine gravel, paired off in two sets of two each, their concave sides facing, and about seven inches distant from each other. Taking an envelope from his pocket the Professor carefully scooped part of the sand into it, then closed the cabinet door and returned to the library.

Approaching the window, which had blown open as the lights went out, he examined its white-enameled sill closely, collected a few grains of sand from it, and bent down to observe the wall and baseboard immediately under it.

His search was rewarded, for, so faint as to be scarcely noticeable, but perceptible to one who knew what he looked for, was a tiny, dirty-yellow stain on the white baseboard, and two more, one about two feet below and ten to eleven inches to the left of the other, against the gray wall paper.

Mentally the Professor blessed his untidy habit of using his pockets for correspondence files as he brushed specimens of these stains into two more envelopes and scribbled identifying notations on each container.

"Now," he informed himself as he knocked the ashes from his pipe into the fire, "we'll have a look around the outside of the house before the police begin to ask embarrassing questions."

The wind was howling like a thousand banshees with ulcerated teeth, lashing the tall, somber cedars, which lined the Milsted driveway, till they bent almost double before its force, and hurling sheets of mingled snow and sleet against the house walls and window panes. The entire north wall of the Milsted mansion was encrusted with storm-castings as the Professor, muffled to the eyes in his motoring coat and with his fur cap pulled well over his ears, forced his way through the tempest to the spot beneath the library window.

"No chance of finding anything here," he admitted reluctantly as he threw the beam of his electric torch against the ice-covered clapboards. "Any traces are as dead as the dodo. You couldn't track an elephant through this storm. I might as well get back to—ah?" He broke his soliloquy short with a sharp, interrogative exclamation as his foot came in contact with some tiny object imbedded in the half-frozen snow.

Dropping to his knees, he played his electric light over the glacial mass at his feet, dug his fingers through the sleet-crust and exhumed a tiny, glistening object about an inch and a half in length and surprisingly heavy for its size. No need to speculate

on the nature of his discovery. The little golden statue, representing a squatting monkey, and exquisitely executed in gold, the face ornamented with rubies, told him at a glance what it was. Hanuman, the Monkey God, was found.

The flashlight's ray disclosed something else. About the spot where the Professor had stumbled over the jewel somebody else had been clawing furiously, for the half-obliterated marks of frantic fingers were plainly visible in the snow. Only desperate haste, biting cold and unrelieved darkness had prevented the other from finding the statuette which the Professor had come upon accidentally.

"Hum," Forrester remarked as he shut off his flashlight and rose, "this is interesting; mighty interesting. Would be worth while trying to find any tracks?"

Two minutes' attempt convinced him it would not. Sheltered from the full fury of the storm by the house, the snow where the monkey's statue had been lost retained the ridges made by the questing fingers which missed what the Professor found; but three feet distant the drifting flakes and lashing sleet obliterated Forrester's own tracks almost as soon as he made them. To seek any person who had passed that way, even a few minutes before, was as bootless an undertaking as attempting to trace a ship across the Atlantic by her wake. "No go," he admitted, after wrestling with the gale for ten yards or so; "better get in and thaw out."

"Find anything?" demanded young Carpenter as the Professor relieved himself of cap and ulster and held his hands to the hall fire, flexing and stretching his fingers to restore circulation.

"Umpf," responded the Professor, bending closer to the blaze and disdaining a glance at his questioner.

"Nut!" muttered Carpenter to the young woman beside him. "Darndest nut I ever saw, racing around in this storm looking for God-knows-what. Reckon the old fool expects to find out why Milsted shot himself?"

If the Professor heard Mr. Carpenter's uncomplimentary remarks he gave no sign of resentment. Turning from the fire as soon as the younger man had withdrawn, he hurried to the library, and with only the corpse of his late host for company, fell to comparing the bits of earth he had salvaged from the steel cabinet, the window sill and the library walls and baseboard.

"Hello, Professor Forrester; what are you doing here?" queried a sharp-featured young man as he entered the library and put a portmanteau down on the table. "Lookin' for traces of the Pyramid-builders?"

Forrester regarded the newcomer sharply through the lenses of his neat, rimless pince-nez. "I don't believe I—" he began, but the other interrupted with a laugh.

"Of course, you don't," he agreed. "I didn't expect you would. I'm Nesbit—Lambert Nesbit, B. S., in '20, and M.D., in '24. Never had any of your classes, but used to see you on the campus and on the platform at commencements."

"Oh!" the Professor responded. "And you're—"

"Yep, I'm the coroner. Practice wasn't goin' any too good when I got out, for I just missed the flu epidemic and folks wouldn't get sick to accommodate me, so I busted into politics and got myself elected to this job. They tell me outside you've been keepin' the nest warm for me."

"I've made a few—er—observations," Forrester admitted. "Have you questioned anybody?"

"I'll say I have," the coroner retorted with a twinkle in his eye. "Got two state troopers to ride herd on 'em, and put 'em through their paces in great shape. Gosh, they're one scared crowd! Everybody agrees Milsted shot himself, but if I asked any one of 'em, 'Why did you kill him?' I'll bet a dollar he'd break down and confess.

"Well"—he turned to the body with a brisk, professional air—"I wonder why the old coot *did* kill himself?"

With the deftness of long practice, covering the repugnance he felt for his task with a running fire of cynical comment, the young physician examined the remains, noted the position of the wound, the pistol in the dead hand and the posture of the body.

"Plain as a pike-staff," he announced, rising and dusting his trousers knees. "Never saw an opener case of suicide in my life, but, as Bobbie Burns would say,

"*'One thing must still be greatly dark,
The reason why he did it.'*"

"I shouldn't be too cock-sure it's suicide if I were you," Professor Forrester replied.

"Eh? The devil you say!" Dr. Nesbit shot him a quick glance. "Why not?"

"Look at that wound again."

"Thanks; I've already had a fine, grandstand view of it. Right through the frontal bone, slick and clean as a whistle."

"But did you see any powder brand around it?" Forrester insisted. "Remember, in the nature of things, Milsted couldn't have held that gun more than a foot from his head, and at that distance, even with smokeless powder, there would have been some burning of the tissues, or at least a scarification of the skin from the powder gases."

"Hum; by the Lord Harry, Professor, you're

right!" the young official admitted. "I overlooked it. Still—"

"Try to take that pistol from his hand," the Professor persisted.

"He's certainly holding it," the coroner admitted as he rose after tugging futilely at the weapon clasped in the dead man's fingers. "*Rigor mortis* set in early—"

"*Rigor* fiddlesticks!" Forrester scoffed. "Feel his jaw and neck, man; that's where the stiffening would begin, if it were *rigor mortis*. You'll find those muscles still flaccid."

"Right you are," Dr. Nesbit agreed as he prodded the dead man's facial muscles with a practiced forefinger. "But how do you account for his grasping that gun so—"

The Professor sighed in exasperation. "Did you ever hear of the condition known as cadaveric spasm?" he asked sharply. "That's a perfect example of it. You know, as a physician—or you ought to, if you don't—that when death takes place suddenly, especially from injury to the nervous system, as in this case, where the brain was pierced, the body, or parts of it, notably the hands, become rigid almost immediately. I remember once coming on the body of a poor chap who'd been murdered in the Gobi desert. Some brigands had shot him through the head from behind as he was in the act of eating a piece of mutton, and, though his body had almost completely mummified when we found him, he was still grasping the sheep bone as if it were a pole of a galvanic battery."

"Right-o," the coroner gave a short, affirmative nod. "Absolutely right, Professor. This man was shot through the brain, too, as you say. But that's one of the surest indicia of suicide, you know. No murderer could put that gun in his hand after killing him and make his fingers grasp it as they do."

"Exactly," Forrester nodded in his turn. "But suppose that instead of shooting himself, Milsted had drawn his gun to shoot at someone else, and actually fired one shot before, or just as, the other potted *him*. What then? Wouldn't we have just the conditions we find here?"

"Yes," Nesbit conceded, "but the facts don't match your theory. Only one shot was heard, and all the testimony, with one exception, is to the effect that there was nobody for Milsted to shoot at, even if there'd been someone to shoot him."

"Right," Forrester replied, "and it's my ward, Miss Osterhaut, who says *Milsted fired toward the window* just before he fell. I'd take her word against a dozen of these scatter-brained young fools' testimony. She has been brought up to observe things, and do it accurately."

"But—"

"And here's something else for you to chew on," the Professor continued, brushing aside the half-uttered protest—"look at these—"

Leading the way to the museum he opened the empty cabinet and directed his companion's gaze to the faint marks on its floor. "Recognize 'em?" he demanded.

"Can't say I do."

"Very well, then. I'll tell you. They're footprints. Somebody who had been walking through the snow, before it was deep enough to cover the ground completely, was standing in that cabinet today. You can make out the heel-and toe-prints of his shoes, and here you can see where the sand and gravel has been spread out in a film over the metal where the snow melted from his boots. It's a glacial silt-deposit in miniature. That dates his visit. It didn't start snowing till nearly six o'clock this afternoon, and the ground was frozen hard as bed-rock up to an hour or so before the storm began. The temperature rose several degrees—enough to thaw the very top of the ground—before the snow commenced, and for the first half-hour or so the flakes were wet. This sleet has been coming down only the last hour, maybe a little less. So I say somebody walked through the snow just after it began, got a scum of sand on his shoes and hid in this case without stopping to wipe his boots. He could stand here and see everything going on in the room through the slits in the cabinet door."

Dr. Nesbit smiled ironically as he shook his head. "You may be able to take a piece of skull and build a man from it, or reconstruct a dinosaur from a splint of thigh-bone, Professor Forrester," he conceded,

"but I'm not ready to admit you've reconstructed a case of burglary and murder here."

"Then look at this," the Professor urged, leading the way back to the library and indicating the wall beneath the window. "This is the window that everybody agrees opened mysteriously just as the lights went out. Now, here on the baseboard, if you'll look closely, you'll find exactly such sand stains as are on the cabinet floor. And here—" he indicated the faint smudges on the wall—"are the foot marks where somebody took a running start, braced his feet first against the board, then the wall, and with his hands holding the window sill, swarmed up and yanked the casement open. And here—" he pointed triumphantly to the sill—"are other marks, not much more than dabs of sand, I'll grant you, but still marks, where the fellow rested his feet on the sill before he started to leap to the ground outside."

"But you're assuming too much," Nesbit objected. "These marks might easily have been made some other way. I know my house is forever getting all sorts of spots and splotches on it, no matter how hard my wife scrubs and dusts."

Forrester snorted in disgust. "Can't you use your eyes at all?" he demanded. "Look at this, and this, and this—" he thrust the envelopes in which his specimens were stored under the coroner's nose—"the sand in each of those envelopes is identical. If the cabinet was stained with yellow sand, and the wall with red and the window sill with black or gray smut, I'd agree with you; but all the stains are made by the same material. I tell you, whoever hid in that cabinet ran from the museum to the library and made his escape through the window when the lights went out! See here, let's prove it. Call everybody who was present when Milsted died and ask them, separately, if they can remember whether or not the library door opened about the same time the confusion preceding the shooting began."

Dr. Nesbit stepped to the door and summoned the six witnesses to the tragedy, admitting them one at a time and asking each the question suggested by the Professor. Rosalie and three others recalled there had been a faint squeak "as though a door was being opened carefully" before Milsted had appeared to go berserker. One of the others thought the museum door had opened a little—"blown by a draft," she assumed—while the sixth witness remembered nothing of the sort.

"That's the best proof in the world that the door did open," the Professor insisted. "If every one of them had agreed it did, we might have assumed your question suggested their answers—human memory is a tricky thing, at best—and that they thought they recalled something which actually didn't happen;

but diverse testimony in such a case is its own best proof."

"'Saul, Saul, almost thou persuadest me,'" Coroner Nesbit protested with a laugh. "Seriously, though, Professor, you've got me thinking. I still believe this is a suicide, but everything you've suggested *could* have happened just as you say—maybe."

"'Maybe' be hanged!" the Professor blazed! "It did, I tell you!"

"But what about Herman, or whatever its name was, that led to the tragedy?" Nesbit asked, half of himself, half of the professor. "As I understand it, Milsted claimed someone had stolen some sort of heathen idol from his museum and was throwing a catch-the-low-down-cuss party when he was—when he shot himself."

"I was coming to that," Forrester answered. "When Mr. Milsted first accused one of us of stealing the statue of Hanuman, I thought he might be indulging in some ill-timed joke, or staging a show with some ulterior motive. He was a queer sort, and I never fancied him very much. But I'm convinced now the jewel really was stolen, and stolen by the person who hid in the cabinet and escaped through the window and murdered Milsted."

"How do you make that out?" Nesbit wanted to know. "Nobody's seen the thief, or the stolen property, for that matter—"

"Oh, yes, somebody has," Forrester corrected, drawing the little golden image with its ruby eyes and nostrils from his pocket and handing it to the astonished coroner. "I found this outside in the snow, directly under that window, just where a person, jumping from that height and landing on slippery ground, might have dropped it. I wish you'd take official charge of it for a few days and tell no one about it till you hear from me."

Briefly he described his search for clues outside the house, the finding of the idol and the finger marks where its loser had made a hurried hunt for it.

"Well, I'll be—this trick is yours, Professor," the young doctor agreed. "I'm still holding to the hypothesis of suicide, but we'll impanel no jury tonight, or until I've had time to perform an autopsy on the body. Can I reach you by phone if I need you?"

"Of course," the Professor assured him.

"All right. I'll take the names and addresses of everyone present, and dismiss 'em, pending the inquest. Whether you're right or wrong, Professor, you've given me more mental gymnastics this evening than I've had since I attended the University." He held out his hand with a genial smile. "Goodnight, sir."

"**L**ambert Nesbit speaking, Professor," a cheerful voice announced at the telephone, shortly after noon the following day. "Pick up the marbles; you win."

"Eh, how's that—" Professor Forrester began, but the coroner was bursting with information and refused to be interrupted.

"I autopsied Milsted's body this morning," he continued, "and everything points to your theory of murder. In fact, it *couldn't* have been suicide. When I removed the skull cap I found a bullet had passed through the frontal bone slightly to the left of the frontal suture, penetrating the left superior frontal lobe of the brain, piercing the proecentral fissure with a downward course, and traveling almost to the horizontal fissure of Sylvinus. Do you get me, or am I too technical?"

"Not at all," Forrester assured him. "Remember, Nesbit, I was studying comparative anatomy, putting in six hours a week in the dissecting room, when you were learning to spin a top and play marbles for keeps. Go on, what else did you find?"

"Well, first off, I realized that it would have been impossible for a man to shoot himself in that manner unless he held the stock of the pistol above the level of his head—I experimented on myself by holding a gun with the muzzle touching my forehead where the wound in Milsted's head was. He might have done it by bracing the barrel against his head and pulling the trigger with his thumb, but, as you demonstrated last night, Milsted was clutching the pistol with the rigidity of a cadaveric spasm, which must have occurred at the moment of death, and his forefinger was on the trigger. There wasn't a Chinaman's chance of his shifting his grip on the stock between the shot and the time death ensued, for he must have died instantly from that wound."

"My boy," Forrester assured him, "I'm beginning to have hopes of you. It was hard to convince you last night, but I'll admit you're not one of those thick-headed zanies who persist in error just for the sake of making fools of themselves."

"Thanks," the coroner replied dryly. "But you ain't heard nothin' yet. When I compared the bullet in Milsted's brain with a cartridge from the magazine of his pistol, I found the lethal missile was a soft lead, conical bullet of about 20-20 caliber, while Milsted's gun is a Lüger and shoots a .25 cupro-nickel-coated bullet. I was talkin' with a lieutenant in the State Constabulary about it today, and he told me those guns have a muzzle velocity of about twelve hundred feet a second, and if Milsted had shot himself with his own gun the bullet would have gone clear through his head and probably through the wall behind him, as well."

"I could have told you that," Forrester replied. "Have you any other information?"

"Not right now; but there's not much doubt Milsted was murdered. What sticks in my craw, though, is who did it, and why, and why the devil didn't anyone hear a second shot? D'ye reckon both parties could have fired at once, so the two reports sounded like one?"

"Um; that's possible," Forrester agreed, "but you'll remember that five of the six witnesses to the tragedy fail to recall seeing anything resembling a man at the window when Milsted died, and they'd not have been apt to miss seeing a pistol flash. No, I don't think—here, wait a minute! How long can you postpone the inquest?"

"Well, there's no limit prescribed by law, but the jury has to be sworn *super visum corporis*—on viewing the body, you know—and we can't keep poor old Milsted above ground indefinitely, waiting to swear in the jury. Tell you what I'll do, if you say. I'll impanel a jury, swear 'em in over the body, and then continue the inquest subject to call. I can get away with that, all right. What were you going to suggest?"

"Take that bullet you found in the brain down to Roach's sporting goods store and have one of their arms experts look at it. I noticed an English air-pistol on display in their window the other day, and it strikes me an air-gun might be the explanation to the whole affair. If the murder had been committed with one of those weapons we'd have about the same amount of mystery we have here, for the thing would probably shoot with practically no sound and would make no flash. These guns are comparatively new in

this country, but I daresay they're fairly well known in the British possessions."

"You think the murderer was an Englishman, then?"

"Not exactly that, but I've got what you'd probably call a 'hunch,' Nesbit."

"Good enough. We'll play it through. I'll see what Roach's man has to say and report later. We can hold the inquest up a week or so if necessary, while we gumshoe around for more dope."

"I don't think we'll need wait that long," the Professor told him, as he hung up the phone and resumed marking a pile of examination papers.

"Missie like buy ve'y pretty fancy work?" a round-faced young man with somnolent eyes, clad in a threadbare overcoat and rather decrepit fez, demanded the following afternoon, when Rosalie answered the ringing of the front doorbell.

"No, I—" the Professor's pretty ward began, then checked her refusal, half spoken, as her large, topaz eyes suddenly narrowed the tiniest fraction of an inch. "Come in," she invited. "I won't promise to buy anything; but I'll look."

"Missie like my t'ings ve'y much," the peddler announced confidently, as he followed her down the hall and into the living room. "See—" he opened an imitation alligator-hide suitcase and displayed the usual stock in trade of the itinerant Armenian huckster—"ve'y pretty, ve'y cheap, Missie. I t'ink you like buy some, mebbe so."

Attracted by the voices, Professor Forrester put down his book and strolled into the living room, leaving the study door open behind him.

"Shopping again?" he asked with a twinkle in his eye.

Rosalie had spent almost a year in occidental freedom since the Professor rescued her from the entourage of a certain villainous half-caste from Singapore, and the avidity with which she conformed to the Western custom of permitting women to buy their own finery had caused the Professor more than a little amusement.

"Yes, Uncle Harvey," she returned, throwing him a radiant smile. "This gentleman says he's from Armenia, and he has some of the loveliest things."

Forrester looked with astonishment from the girl to the mass of miscellaneous horrors spread on the floor. Even a layman could see these alleged Madeira and Normandy scarves and Egyptian table covers were of the home-brewed variety, the sort which are stamped out, thousands at a time, by machinery in New Jersey, and foisted on a credulous public by smooth-spoken knaves from the Levant.

The Professor, who knew the home industries of every people in the world as well as he understood their dialects, could recognize the counterfeits with one eye closed, and Rosalie, who had spent ten years of her life in the heart of the East should certainly have been the last one to be deceived by such crude forgeries. Yet there she stood, apparently enraptured, and begged the vendor to display more of his atrocities.

"This ve'y ni-ce piece work," that worthy commended, throwing a cotton cloth thickly encrusted with machine embroidery over his right arm so that it swathed him from shoulder to wrist. "This made 'specially for ladies who like ni-ce t'ings."

His stock patter swept rapidly on, detailing the manifold perfections of the luncheon cloth, but his sleepy eyes traveled round the room, glanced through the open door of the study, and rested on a tiny brass paper weight which stood on the Professor's desk. The knick-knack was an inexpensive piece of Japanese work, executed in polished brass, and represented a diminutive monkey in the act of holding his paws before his mouth—one of the familiar "speak no evil" symbols to be found in every curio store. Just then it glittered in a ray of the afternoon sun as though it were burnished gold instead of hammered brass. The young man's eyes shone with a sudden fierce light of jubilation as they encountered the toy, and he moved a step nearer the study door.

"Ye-es, this ve'y ni-ce cover for ni-ce lady's table—" he drawled, fumbling in the side pocket of his overcoat beneath the cotton cloth which still draped his arm.

Darwaza bundo!" Rosalie exclaimed shrilly.

The peddler started as though stung by a yellow-jacket, his right arm writhing under the covering of the sheet of embroidery like a snake beneath a blanket.

With a furious movement he whipped the cloth from his shoulder, wrenched something from his pocket and wheeled, backing toward the study with long, cautious steps.

"Look out, Uncle Harvey!" Rosalie's warning came sharply. Next instant she launched herself across the room like a fury, rushing between the Armenian and the astonished Professor.

"Dog, son of filth, unworthy offspring of a he-goat and a bad smell!" she spat at the hawker in a torrent of Hindustani, her amber eyes glowing balefully, her lovely mouth distended like that of an angry cat.

There was a flash of steel in the afternoon sunlight, something like a flickering flame leaped to life in the girl's right hand and swept forward and down like a cracking whiplash. The peddler screamed with amazement and pain and dropped the object he had half drawn from his pocket.

Rosalie's slim, silk-and-satin-shod foot shot out, kicking the thing out of reach as she menaced the wounded huckster with a ten-inch, wavy-bladed Malay *kris*.

"Tie him up, Uncle Harvey," she bade, thrusting her knife forward to within an inch of the Armenian's belt buckle, then, to the peddler, "Stand still, grandson of a toad, or by the Three Holy Ones, I shall slit your unclean throat and pour forth your vile blood as an offering to Kali!" The peddler followed her advice to the letter, though his frightened glance turned this way and that, any direction but toward the girl's fierce eyes and the glittering, razor-sharp blade of her dagger.

Seizing a length of lace from the open suitcase, Forrester hastily twisted it into a rope and trussed the huckster's elbows behind him—a far more effective manner of binding than strapping the wrists together—then tore a length from one of the cotton embroideries and bandaged the fellow's wounded wrist.

"Sit down," he ordered curtly, motioning the captive to a chair; then to Rosalie: "I hope you know what you're about, young woman. If you've run amuck, we're in for a tidy little lawsuit, if not for a criminal prosecution."

"Hou!" Rosalie laughed, lapsing into oriental vernacular, which she still did under the stress of excitement. "Behold, my lord, what your slave has discovered." With a quick fillip, she removed the fez from the peddler's head, displaying a small device in red painted on his forehead near the hairline.

It was a small crescent which nearly enclosed a tiny disc within its horns, and Forrester started at the sight. "Good heavens!" he exclaimed. "Why, it's the caste mark of a follower of Siva!"

"Yes, my lord, it is nothing less," the girl replied with a triumphant smile. "When this base-born descendant of a hyena and a mangy female monkey appeared at my master's house, wishing to show me his detestable wares, I was about to send him on his way, but the day is warm for winter and he put up his hand to wipe his brow, so that I did behold the caste mark for an instant as he put back his cap. Many an Armenian have I seen—we had hundreds of them in Singapore—but never have I beheld one who wore the sign of Siva.

"Then I did remember, master of my life, how the villainous Chandra Roi (may the vultures devour his eyeballs!) sometimes hired these Siva fellows to do his filthy work when even the Chinamen would not, and I knew this one came to my master's house for no good.

"Two nights ago when Milsted Sahib spoke of the loss of his image of Hanuman, the others knew not what he referred to, but you and I, my lord, knew that Hanuman is the Monkey God of the people of Hind, and though in this land the monkey dances to the music of hand organs, in India he is a very sacred beast.

"I knew, too, that Milsted Sahib was killed by someone, for did I not behold him shooting at a thing which perched in his window-place, as though Hanuman himself had come to claim his image? And was he not himself shot down? Men do not die from bullets from their own guns when those guns are pointed away from them.

"Also I knew that you went outside the house after the murder, and, though the others saw nothing when you returned, Mumtaz Banjjan dwells in the shadow of her lord's bounty, and his every mood is as plain to her as print upon a book's page. She could see he was excited, and also pleased by something he had found, and there was no further mention of the stolen god. Therefore Mumtaz Banjjan placed herself near the door while her master and the Doctor Sahib talked in the library, and overheard much which passed between them. She knew he had found the god and given it to the young Nesbit, and she heard of the marks of some other person's search for that same idol in the snow. All these things Mumtaz treasured in her memory, and when she beheld the mark of Siva upon this accursed one's brow she bethought her that he must have seen her master pick up the god and take it into the house with him. Therefore, she thought, this one had come here to steal the god back, perhaps to murder her master as he also murdered Milsted Sahib. So she did invite

him into the house with fair words that she might watch him, and she saw his unholy eyes light upon the little monkey of brass in the room where my lord reads from great books and writes on paper, which he, being but a pig and an ignorant fellow, doubtless mistook for the very god he stole from Milsted Sahib. And when she saw him reach into his pocket beneath the cloth he held upon his arm she knew he sought some weapon.

"So Mumtaz cried out '*Darwaza bundo*' which, as my lord knows, means only 'shut the door,' in Hindustani; but it was enough. The lowborn one recognized the words, and betrayed himself, and Mumtaz cut his wicked hand before he could do injury to the master who holds both her body and her soul as lightly in his hand as a child holds a rattle."

"Um; so I see," Forrester commented, "and a very neat piece of work you did, too, my dear. But you might have been shot."

"Forrester Sahib is Mumtaz Banjjan's master, and Mumtaz Banjjan is his slave," the girl replied, lowering her head humbly. "He is the light of her eyes and the breath of her nostrils and the blood of her heart. What does it matter if the slave dies, so the master lives?"

"Never mind the compliments," Professor Forrester waved his hand wearily. He had long since given up trying to convince Rosalie that she must not call herself his slave. "Just at present I require information. How is it you had that *kris* so handy?"

Rosalie's—or Mumtaz Banjjan's—face lit with a smile. "I belong to my lord, the mighty Forrester Sahib," she announced primly, "if he chooses not to salute my lips I shall go to my grave unkissed; but there are certain young men who think not so. In Singapore I learned that the kris is a sharp tongue which argues well; therefore, when the young men urge me to do what they call 'pet,' if I cannot rebuff them with my laughter or my hands, I wear that which will convince them. The American clothes are clumsy for such a purpose—I cannot wear the knife at my belt—therefore I conceal it in the back of my dress, between my shoulders."

"You little savage!" Professor Forrester chuckled, as he stooped to recover the pistol she had kicked into the corner of the room. Whimsically, he remembered that certain desperadoes of the early Wild West were wont to conceal their Bowie knives in the collars of their coats, and wondered what effect Rosalie's sudden production of a murderous Malay short sword would have at some afternoon tea.

He held the captured pistol to the light and examined it closely. It was a heavy, blue steel weapon with a thick barrel upon which a smaller calibered tube was set. By breaking the stock, after the manner of a revolver, a plunger was withdrawn from the larger barrel, and when the stock was jammed back in place the plunger was thrust into the tube again, compressing sufficient air in the chamber to drive a light bullet with a velocity equal to that of a black-powder pistol. Across the stock was engraved the word Lübeck.

"H'm," the Professor commented, trying the weapon's mechanism, "German make, eh? I might have known they'd have a model on the market as soon as the British perfected one. Well, I think we've about all the evidence necessary for Nesbit's inquest.

"Rosalie," he turned to the girl, "just stand watch over our prisoner while I telephone the police, will you?"

As he retired to the study to notify the authorities he heard the extraordinary young woman informing her captive that a single false move on his part would result in instant and complete disembowelment.

"Now," the Professor bent a stern gaze on the peddler, "why did you come here?"

The pseudo-Armenian shrugged his shoulders, or came as near doing it as was possible while his elbows were bound behind him, and tightly lashed to the rungs of a chair-back.

"I am a follower of Hanuman," he replied in perfect English. "The grandfather of the man I put to death stole the image of our god from its temple in India almost a hundred years ago and kept it in his house for sacrilegious fools to gape at. Copies of the god's image may be bought in the bazaars throughout India, and this we cannot prevent, but to have our sacred relics ravished from our temples—suppose *we* should come to your land and take from off your altars the images of your plaster saints, or the little pieces of bread which you worship, how would you feel about it? Other Englay have stolen other statues of the god from us, and we have hunted them down, one at a time, taken back our own and—their lives. The Milsted whom I killed—thieving son of a thieving grandsire that he was!—was the last. Others of our company had accounted for the rest; Milsted was mine."

"Um?" Forrester nodded thoughtfully. "How did you get into the house?"

The Hindu smiled sardonically. "That was not hard to one of my calling," he answered. "There was a great company of fools assembled at the place, and I bribed one of the servants to tell me the location of the room where Hanuman was kept. While all were at dinner I climbed through the library window and entered the museum. The god was not in any of the glass cases, but I found him in the safe, for it was an old-fashioned one and the lock was easy to pick. When I heard anyone near I hid in a steel case which happened to be empty. When I had taken the statue from the safe, but before I could get away, Milsted came to the museum and discovered his loss. I would have shot him then, but there was someone in the next room, and I feared he would raise the alarm. When Milsted found the god was gone he ran out and called more people, and I thought they were coming to take me, but before any could enter the room where I hid the lights went out and I ran through the dark to the window which I had left unlocked, and was preparing to jump to the ground when Milsted saw me and tried to kill me.

"I shot him with the gun which makes no sound and dropped to the ground, but slipped on the snow and lost the image. There was no time to stay and search for it, for the house was roused, so I ran to the barn and hid, watching the spot where I had dropped Hanuman. After a time I saw someone looking about the ground beneath the window, and saw him pick something up and put it in his pocket. By the light from the window I recognized you, Forrester Sahib, and followed you here to take back that which was mine, and kill you, too, if I could, for you have profaned Hanuman by your touch."

"Why, you didn't think I'd *keep* the thing, did you?" the Professor asked in amazement.

The Indian shrugged again. "You are an *Englay*," he answered. "Whether the *Englay* steal from each other I do not know, but that they steal from us I know very well. Also I have heard that you are one of those who despoil even the tombs of the dead in the name of science. How should I know whether you would keep that which you found when you thought no one watched?"

"Uncle Harvey," Rosalie interrupted, "this man is a liar. He says he is a follower of Hanuman, but we have seen the sign of Siva on him, and know him for a Dakait—one whose trade and religion is murder and robbery. His talk of recovering the god for his temple is a lie. He would sell it, if he could get it; maybe to the priests of the temple from which it was stolen, but certainly he would sell it."

She turned to the pinioned Indian and hurled a torrent of fluent, though none too polite, Hindustani at him. "Dishonorable son of a shameless mother," she exclaimed, "confess that you came not to return Hanuman to his home, but to steal him for yourself. I know your kind. You are a brother to the weasel and blood-brother to the snake. In the night you creep into the houses of honest men and they die and you possess their goods. Say, is it not for the honor of Kali, goddess of thieves, that you have done this thing?"

The man stared at her in pop-eyed astonishment. That a fair-haired young lady of the Occident should speak idiomatic Hindustani, even to a liberal use of the intimate insults without which no unfriendly conversation is complete in that tongue, astonished him almost as much as the girl's deft handling of her *kris* had done a few minutes before.

"It is true," he acknowledged, with a fatalistic writhing of his shoulders. "Of what avail to lie to one who possesses the beauty of the moonflower and the wisdom of the serpent? It is even as you have said."

Rosalie preened herself like a satisfied bird. "You do well to call me moonflower, who was known by that name for many years," she announced.

"Uncle Harvey," she resumed her rather shaky English as she addressed the Professor, though she was perfectly aware he spoke Hindustani as well as she did, "I think they will make no mistake when they hang this fellow. He is one dam' bad egg."

Adventure THRILLS!

WHEN ONLY 13 YEARS OLD RICHARD E. BYRD ALONE TRAVELED AROUND THE WORLD

VISITING MANY COUNTRIES AND EXPERIENCING MANY ADVENTURES.

WHILE IN THE PHILIPPINES YOUNG BYRD WENT RIDING ALONG A RIVER AND WAS ATTACKED BY A BAND OF LADRONES WHO WERE ARMED WITH SHARP BOLOS. FLOURISHING AN OLD ARMY REVOLVER—WHICH HE DID NOT KNOW HOW TO SHOOT— DICK FRIGHTENED THE REBELS AS HE PLUNGED HIS HORSE INTO THE STREAM AND ESCAPED.

FOUGHT DUEL 210 TIMES!

CAPTAIN FOURNIER AND MAJOR DUPONT, RIVAL FRENCH OFFICERS, BEGAN A DUEL IN STRASSBURG IN 1794 AND AFTER 210 COMBATS—DURING WHICH EACH DUELIST WAS WOUNDED OVER 40 TIMES—THE AFFAIR WAS FINALLY ENDED IN NEVILLY IN 1813 WHEN DUPONT WAS KILLED.

36 COUNTRIES VISITED BY GLOBE TROTTER

GREGORY MASON WHO DURING 1922-3 LED AN EXPEDITION EXPLORING CENTRAL AMERICA WHERE HE LOCATED THE RUINS OF THE "LAST CITIES OF THE MAYAS."

SCALED 38 OF WORLD'S HIGHEST PEAKS IN A SINGLE SUMMER!

GEORGIA ENGELHARD, OF NEW YORK, DARING MOUNTAIN CLIMBING ADVENTURER, SET A NEW WOMEN'S ENDURANCE RECORD CHAMPIONSHIP BY SCALING 38 PEAKS INCLUDING MT. ASSINIBOINE (11,878 FEET) IN THE CANADIAN ROCKIES.

ADVENTURE
by Clark Ashton Smith

*Let us leave the hateful town
With its stale, forgotten lies;
Far beneath renewing skies,
Where the piny slope goes down,
All with April love and laughter—
None to leer and none to frown—
We shall pass and follow after
Shattered lace of waters spun
On a steep and stony loom
Down the depths of laurel-gloom.
Finding there a world re-made
In the fern-embowered shade,
Weaving bright oblivion
Still from frailest blossom-trove,
We shall mix our wilding love
With the woodland and the sun.*

*Let us loiter, hand in hand,
Hearing but the heart's command,
Half our steps by kisses stayed,
Prove the spring-enchanted glade;
Breast to breast and limb to limb,
Seize our happiness and bind it—
Lose the pulse of time and find it,
Free as vagrant seraphim.
Ever leave regret and rue
To the dutiful and jealous
Fools that are not near to tell us
All the things we should not do.*

*Though the bedded ferns be broken,
And dishevelled blossoms lie
On the rumpled moss for token
Of the day's mad errantry—
Still the tacit pines will keep
Darkly in their sighing sleep
All the sweet and perilous story;
And the oaks and willows hoary
For unheeding ears will tell
Only things ineffable;
And the later eyes that look
On the pool-delaying brook,
Shall not see within its glass
Two that came to kiss and pass.*

DOUBLE-SHUFFLE

by Edwin Baird

Sammy the tramp owned a discontent—a perplexing, irritating discontent. At a sloppy table in his favorite Chicago saloon he sat and scowled and essayed self-analysis. But it was no use. His distemper eluded diagnosis.

He lowered his head, glared sullenly at his glass, and in a low voice swore so vividly that his pot-companion, sitting opposite, was moved to a pipe of to-

bacco and compassionate utterance.

"Why, Sammy," he asked with brotherly concern, "what's bitin' you, pal? I declare, you're a cross between a mildewed squash and G. Bernard Shaw eatin' pickles and lemons. Come, why so pensive—"

"Aw, freeze up," growled Sammy, "and have another drink," he added penitently.

He motioned to the bartender and from a pocket of his patched and grimy trousers plucked a wad of ragged money the size of his wrist. This occasioned no riot. Since it was *on dit* in lower Clark Street circles that an uncompromising switch-engine had recently sent Sammy to a St. Louis hospital, that a compromising claim agent had given him three hundred dollars, and that about one hundred and fifty dollars of this sum yet remained with him, the barroom foregathering evinced no surprise at the plethoric display.

But a trembling, whisky-crazed wretch, who had just entered, noticed, and his watery eyes glistened with a feverish anticipation. With timorous humility he sidled to the table, sat down, and looked meekly, pleadingly at the wealthy one.

Silently Sammy pushed back his chair and rose. Irately he pointed to the door.

"Get out o' here!" he roared. "You and your greasy leer. Get out, you—you—rat! Quick, or I'll bounce this booze-jug off your knob."

He seized the bottle from the returning bartender. The intruder hastily departed, upsetting two or three chairs *en route*. Sox surveyed his comrade in meek wonder.

"Sammy," he began timidly after the excitement had subsided, "what—"

"I'll tell you what!" blazed Sammy, leaning across the table with right fist clenched. "I'm sick of this"—he waved his left hand around the smutty barroom. "I'm sick of associatin' with pigs like you; I'm sick of not seein' and knowin' nobody but a lot of ragged guys who don't do nothin' but soak up cheap booze and sleep and cuss. I'm sick of it all—see?"

He glanced contemptuously at his auditor, then moved his chair round and turned his back.

Somewhere below the unwashed surface of Sox's poltroonery smoldered a spark of spunk. It flared up now defiantly.

"And who are you," he cried hotly, "to talk about ragged pigs! What're you, I'd like to know. You're a fine-lookin' swell, ain't you! Huh!" He spat vigorously. "A fine-lookin' swell! You look like a last year's scarecrow daubed wit' mud—"

He stopped, awed by his own temerity and the fact that Sammy had risen and was standing over him threateningly.

But the next second the malcontent had turned away and was striding toward the swinging doors. Near the end of the bar a group of frowsy men hailed and surrounded him jovially, but drew back as he made no response and let him pass in peace.

Several blocks down the street he stopped and sardonically eyed his reflection in a full-length mirror of a corner haberdasher's. Not a very prepossessing reflection, modish reader, as you shall see.

From top to bottom thus: Hat of a derby species and an obsolete vintage, cracked and rusty its crown, and from its disjointed brim straggles of unkempt hair curling up over ears caked with the grime of many cities; the face as seamed and swollen as a twelve-cent chuck steak and thickly covered with a dark-red beard hacked to a convenient length with a pocket-knife; the eyes, faintly suggesting a bygone pride and intelligence, bloodshot from many potations; in lieu of linen, a greasy undershirt, insufficiently concealed by a buttonless waistcoat, faded and soiled beyond surmisal of its original pattern; the coat of a different hue; the trousers of another still; and woefully shielding his naked feet, shoes ragged and torn and precariously held together by wire and bits of twine.

Not in many years had Sammy seen a mirror larger than his hand, and now that he deliberately viewed himself from tattered tile to battered boot, an intense self-disgust welled up within him and he despised and loathed himself. He wheeled round suddenly, looked up and down the street, and strode savagely toward a brilliantly lighted hostelry in the next block.

A minute later Sammy the tramp, who for the greater part of his twenty-six years of life had shunned bathtubs as though they were vats swarming with rattlesnakes, was descending a marble staircase at the top of which blazed this sign:

TURKISH BATHS

An hour later, having meanwhile dispatched a messenger and twenty dollars to the corner haberdashery, he got into a barber's chair and ordered everything from shoe-shine to shampoo. From the barbershop he went to a unique establishment in State Street, where, on short notice, one could be supplied with all the proper habiliments for evening wear. Silk hat, gloves, pumps, full-dress, all could be supplied while you waited—one hour.

So, after this space had elapsed, there stepped from this swift-aid-to-the-hurried firm a gentleman eminently correct in every detail, even to Inverness cape, gold-headed cane, and Turkish cigarette. His face was not unlike that of the average man of the world; its marks of dissipation had been softened, if not eradicated, by the barber's massage; the mouth and chin were firm and well-shaped; his fingers carefully manicured; his hair freshly trimmed. And in a pocket of his white pique waistcoat was a crumpled ten-dollar bill—all he had in the world.

Probably not the keenest of his associates could have pierced the masquerade and discerned beneath its elegance Sammy the tramp.

As he stood there, drawing on his gloves with a leisurely air, a shambling object, shivering in rags, dropped from the hurrying street throng, slouched dejectedly a few feet away, then shuffled over and touched his arm

"Can't you help us a bit, sir?" whined the object piteously. "S'help me, I'm starvin', sir. I ain't eat nothin' in forty-eight hours—" The rest was lost in a meaningless mumble.

Without hesitation Sammy reached for the crumpled tenner. But quite as quickly changed his mind and interviewed his new watch.

Then he buttoned his coat, switched his cane up under his arm, and nodded to the beggar.

"Come on," he said. "We'll dine together."

CHAPTER II

At about the same moment Sammy was swearing at Sox in the saloon, one of two young men sitting in the library of a handsome home two miles away was acting rather uncivilly toward the other. His name was Hathaway Allison, and he belonged to a family rich enough to hire a professional genealogist to trace its lineage back to a tadpole.

"Are you asleep, Hathaway?" politely inquired his guest, who had repeated another question three times without eliciting even a monosyllabic response. "If you are, just say so, and I'll quietly withdraw and leave you to your slumbers. I'm not exactly fond of hanging round where I'm not wanted, you know."

Young Allison fidgeted impatiently and looked up with a little frown of annoyance.

"Oh, chop it, Bobby. No, I don't know anything about—about what you asked me about."

A servant entered and lighted the lamps. As the thickening dusk vanished before the soft light, Bobby gave a little gasp of astonishment and leaned forward, staring wonderingly at his friend's face.

"Well, great Dowie!" he exclaimed as soon as the servant had gone. "What're you doing to your face? I'll bet you haven't shaved in a week."

"You lose," said Allison quickly. "Three weeks."

"And your hair! Hathaway, have you boycotted the barbers, or what?"

Hathaway laughed nervously, snipped the end

from a cigar, lighted it, took three or four puffs, flung it in the fire, then rose and locked all the doors.

He returned to his seat and his puzzled visitor, and for several seconds sat with brows knitted thoughtfully, tapping his fingers on the arms of his chair.

"Bobby," he said suddenly, "I think I'm going to tell you something—something I've kept secret a great many years. But I can't keep it any longer, and I've got to tell somebody, and it may as well be you."

"'Twas a dark and stormy night,'" reminded Bobby reprovingly. "But go ahead."

"Some stage thunder and lightning or a little sobby music," agreed Allison good-naturedly, "would not be inappropriate. For what I am about to reveal, Bobby, is as theatric as it is sensational; and I assure you it is sensational as a twenty-cent melodrama. Of course, I may rely upon your absolute secrecy. It won't get past you."

He paused.

"Go on, please."

"Bobby"—his voice lowered, he leaned over and looked his hearer steadily, solemnly in the eye—"Bobby, my name is not Hathaway Allison."

Bobby moved uneasily.

"The man and woman whom everybody thinks are my father and mother are not related to me in any way whatsoever."

Bobby stood up impatiently.

"What the deuce is the matter with you today, Hathaway? You're as creepy as a ghost professor. Go chop those whiskers off and cheer up. You look worse than a Kansas politician after a grasshopper plague."

"No, Bobby, the whiskers stay. Shaggy hair, too. I'm going back, Bobby—back where I belong. And"—he brought his clenched fist heavily down upon his knee—"I'm going back tonight."

"What're you talking about? Going back where?"

Allison settled himself comfortably and lighted a cigarette.

"Well, Bobby, it'll sound melodramatic, as I said before; but I'll condense and cut the pathos. At the precocious age of six or thereabouts, the real Hathaway Allison was lost, strayed, or stolen. I believe there was quite a turmoil at the time. But possibly you've heard of the case—have you?"

"Of course. Mother's told me a dozen times. Wasn't there a mole, or a strawberry mark, or something or other—"

"There was a scar—a deep, bright red scar—in the shape of a 'V' on the right forearm. But to get on with the story. As you know, a frantic search was started; fabulous rewards offered; detectives the world over did their worst. All to no purpose. Several years passed and the topic was forgotten.

"Then suddenly there was a great flourish and a beating of tom-toms, and it was announced to the world that Hathaway Allison was found. Congratulations, poor relations, neighbors, and reporters swarmed in. The newspapers raved, the populace cheered, all was happiness. The poor kid was exhibited, kissed, hugged, and photographed in twenty different attitudes."

The speaker paused abruptly, crossed to the window, stood looking out at turbulent Lake Michigan. After a minute or so he resumed his seat, and in a voice curiously altered, went on: "And the odd part of it all, Bobby, is that Hathaway Allison never was found. Never has been found, and, I am inclined to believe, never will be found."

"Then how the—"

"The day of the hullaballoo there toddled into the kitchen of this house a poor, ragged youngster of nine or ten and asked for food. It seemed he was a sort of mascot of a gang of tramps, who sent him out to beg.

"The Allisons had been heart-broken since the loss of their child; little Hathaway and the embryo vagabond were not dissimilar in appearance; eyes and hair were almost alike. You may guess the rest."

He cleared his throat, shrugged his shoulders, and ended briefly: "Well, I was the kid, that's all."

Bobby's harsh laugh broke the ensuing silence.

"Well, Well! Why all this emotion? You're not the only adopted son in Chicago. The town's full of 'em."

"Yes, I know; but—oh, I'm tired of all this"—he gestured round the luxurious room. "I know it sounds eccentric, but I'm tired of it, all the same— wealth and all that goes with it. I guess it's in the blood.

"Along about this time of the spring I usually get the 'call.' Heretofore I've always turned a deaf ear. But this time I'm going to answer. They're in Europe now. And I'm going away tonight."

Bobby snorted derisively and picked up his hat and gloves.

"Now, Hathaway, forget all this rubbish and put on your things and come with me to a barbershop. Afterward we'll have dinner together. My car's outside, you know. Come on."

But Hathaway smiled and shook his head.

"No use, my boy. I'm through."

"Bosh! You're not a second Count Tolstoy, I hope. Are you coming?"

"No."

"Very well. Goodnight."

"I guess it's good-by, Bobby."

"See you at the club tomorrow," called Bobby from the hall. "Good night."

When his guest had gone, Allison went to his room, closed the door, and took from the wardrobe a suitcase, which he opened upon the bed. It contained a pair of rusty shoes, rustier trousers, frayed waistcoat and threadbare coat, and a sooty cap much too large.

With racing heart and trembling fingers, he stripped to his undergarments and donned the base attire. Afterward he knotted a faded bandana round his neck, pulled the cap low upon his brow, and surveyed himself in the mirror.

Though obviously pleased with the effect, he stuffed the cap in a pocket, donned a derby, and cloaked his rags in a long overcoat before leaving the house, thus occasioning no undue curiosity among the servants.

Several blocks away he disappeared down a dark alley.

When some while later a dusty and seedy-looking tramp carrying a large newspaper bundle walked along the Rush Street bridge, the sharpest pair of eyes among Hathaway Allison's acquaintances would have given him scarcely more than a passing glance.

In the center of the bridge he stopped, glanced quickly round, and stealthily consigned his burden to the black water below. Then he made for State Street, and was swallowed up in the bustling, scrambling, six-o'clock crowds.

Presently, like a rambling derelict, he drifted out of the rushing stream into the harbor of a large doorway.

A sudden impulse had come over him. He would put his disguise to the test.

Affecting a woebegone attitude, he eyed furtively from beneath the weathered visor of his cap a well-dressed man of about his own age who stood a few feet away drawing on his gloves.

At length he slouched over to the prosperous-looking one, laid a pleading hand on his broad-clothed arm, and muttered a supplication for alms.

CHAPTER III

The diners had reached the coffee-cigars-conversational stage of dinner, and chatty discourse was meet.

At his benefactor's request, the shabby one held forth at length on the life of the road. He poured forth in a jargon wondrous to hear. He considered it the vernacular of trampdom.

He enthused over vagabondage; he painted it in glowing colors; he indulged in remarkable superlatives; and when at last he had finished he was

amazed at his power of imagination.

So amazed, indeed, that he failed to notice that his listener was staring at him rather curiously, as though puzzled about something.

"Your story," he said, resting his elbow on the table and turning his cigar thoughtfully between his fingers, "is pretty interesting—in a way. But don't you think it sounds a little fishy? Your language, now—it's just a little too funny to be natural."

He leaned suddenly across the table and looked his guest squarely in the eye.

"How long have you been a 'bo?" he asked sharply. "Who are you, anyhow?"

Young Allison turned pale beneath his ragged beard. It was a critical moment. Happily, the waiter saved it by arriving with the dinner-check. The bill amounted to nine dollars and forty cents. As the host handed the servitor a crumpled ten-dollar bill and waved him away, the guest rose hurriedly and put on his hat.

"Well, good-by, cap'n," he stammered nervously. "I enjoyed de big dine immense. Good-by, good-by!"

He backed away a few steps, then turned and hurried swiftly out of the restaurant.

When he reached the street he stopped and rubbed his cheek thoughtfully.

"Now, who is that chap, I wonder?" he asked himself. "He certainly talked and acted queer. Not been used to money long, that's plain. I wonder who he is."

He gave it up, and turned aimlessly into Randolph Street. A light snow was beginning to fall. The theater crowds were arriving. He stopped before one of the playhouses and mingled in the crush around the *foyer*. Life, color, gaiety, were all round him. But he was an outcast.

An automobile rolled up to the curb, and a man and a woman whom he knew alighted. As they crossed the street he stepped deliberately in front of them. But neither noticed him. He was an outcast.

He walked on down to the corner. A troubled expression clouded his face. Automatically he felt in his coat-pocket for his cigar-case. Then, remembering, laughed shortly and buttoned up his ragged coat.

The snow was growing heavier. Some of it seeped under his collar and trickled down his back. The wind tore at his thin garments angrily. He shivered. The troubled expression deepened. Carriages and autos were now congesting the street. The theater rush was at its height.

Suddenly a change seemed to come over him. He straightened up.

"I guess Bobby's right," he muttered aloud. "Yep." He nodded his head; and, with final conviction: "Yep, he's right. I'm a coward. I can't do it."

He cut across the street to a cab-stand.

The jehu regarded his prospective fare sapiently from his throne.

"Well, not tonight, old skeezicks," he said good-naturedly. "I'm not running a Hinky Dink charity, line this year. But here's a dime for you, anyway."

Young Allison pocketed the dime without smiling. Then he reached inside his waistcoat, ripped out a canvas wallet sewed therein, and took from it a thick sheaf of currency. He gave a five-dollar bill and an address to the cabby, who recovered from his astonishment only enough to drive his strange fare to the north side.

Outside the restaurant, Sammy paused. It was snowing heavily.

The gorgeous door-flunkey approved him with an envious eye; a waiting taxi chauffeur watched him hopefully; an earnest mendicant approached with his plea; and an ambitious policeman, anxious to curry favor, bustled up importantly when Sammy, mindful of his empty pockets, growled a curt refusal.

He watched the beggar slink away before the cop's threatening baton. Then he, looked down and scratched the back of his neck as though somewhat perplexed.

"Now, I wonder who that guy was," he murmured. "Not a moodier, and that's certain. Gee, he was a funny gink!"

Round the corner he reached up, ripped off the high collar which had been torturing him all evening, flung it from him, peeled off his gloves, and cast them after the collar.

A few minutes later the bewhiskered proprietor of one of those wretched, filthy, second-hand clothing shops which infest lower Clark Street was moved to much friction-making with his palms by a fastidious-looking young man who entered the hovel and offered to trade the clothes he wore for some cheap cast-off garments and a cash consideration.

As the odd patron removed his coat and cuff-links and pushed back the sleeves of his shirt, a deep "V"-shaped scar on his right forearm glowed bright red in the light of the sputtering gas-jet.

EVERY MAN A KING

by E. Hoffmann Price

"**D**o you have to go? At this hour?" Olajai turned from her mirror, but did not leave off unfastening the red velvet hood whose twinkling pendants trailed past her cheeks, and to her shoulders. "Couldn't it wait till tomorrow?"

Timur frowned, which made it all the more cer-

tain that the King Maker's granddaughter had not married him for his looks. He snatched a shirt of link mail from a hook, and as he worked it down over his broad shoulders, he grumbled, "One of Bikijek's pets, and he's got the king's seal. Either be a good dog, or run out and join your brother at Saghej

Well!"

Olajai said, wistfully, as she wiped off the last bit of dead-white makeup, "And I thought it'd be lovely, living in Samarkand."

Olajai was shapely of body, and exquisite of face; the Turki heritage, showing in the peach blow tinge of her cheeks, gave features whose every line was sharp and clean and delicate in its drawing. This was Timur's first and only wife, and thus far, he was glad that there were no others.

Though not quite twenty-seven, he looked older, for mountain blizzards and desert blasts had weathered his flat face. Wind blown sand and storm driven sleet had set the Mongol slant of his eyes in a permanent squint; and for all the blue Zaytuni silk tunic he put on over his shirt of linked mail, and his gold embroidery boots, and plumed pork pie hat, he seemed out of place in a palace.

"I'll get away as soon as I can," he promised, and limped out.

Bow legged, and never built for walking, he was further handicapped by an ankle which had stopped a well-aimed arrow. In the tiled reception room, he said to the waiting official, "Something important going on?"

The square-rigged Kipchak did not answer; he merely tapped the big four-cornered seal. In the court, a sleepy groom held his horse, and Timur's.

They skirted the plaza of splendid Samarkand. The bitter clear moon brought out the blue of tile-fronted palaces, and the golden crests of tall minarets. Samarkand, the jewel of the Jagatai Empire, was now the prize of the Kipchak Horde who had overrun the land: and Timur was weary of serving invaders. But for luck, and a friend at Elias Koja's court, he might be an exile, like Olajai's brother, Mir Hussein. Yet, though his position as administrator of affairs gave plenty of enemies and little satisfaction, it at least enabled him to stand between Bikijek's rapacious clique of nobles, and his own conquered neighbors.

Timur trailed the official, instead of riding boot to boot. There was more than just the matter of rank involved. Then, wary ever since that first strange warning, he noted the stirring in the shadows of the archway to the left. Here the street was narrow; here he and his guide faced a cold, white moon.

A bowstring twanged, the strident note of a horseman's bow. Timur ducked. His sword was half unsheathed when the arrow thumped home, nailing the Kipchak squarely in the throat. The fellow made a choking sound, and lurched from the saddle.

Timur wheeled, chin in, and crouching low, so that there was hardly a vulnerable spot exposed. The Ferghana stallion stretched out in a great bound;

hooves struck fire. When things happened too fast for thought, Timur Bek was driven by the instinct to close in, to cut down.

Then a man came out, barefoot, and bearded. "Go home, Timur Bek. There was no other way to warn you."

The face was in shadow, but Timur recognized the voice and the figure. "Good shooting, for a scholar! Why?"

"Allah will enlighten you. Also, the man you were following won't be able to tell anyone you've been enlightened."

"What is this, Kaboul?"

"If all is well with your family, then this is a mistake. And the peace upon you."

Kaboul the Darvish turned into the shadows of the archway. On the ground, Timur saw a horseman's bow, but neither quiver nor arrows.

"One man one arrow."

And now Kaboul was going back to his cubicle to write a Persian quatrain, or an ode in Turki!

Timur, retracing his course, held his horse to a walk, for in spite of the menace which threatened Olajai he could not risk the sound of galloping. When he finally reached the wicket which gave entrance to the rear court of his house, he hitched himself up and stood in the saddle. Then, catching the crown of the wall, he swung himself to the top, and dropped to the grass inside. His first move was to unbolt the little gate, and lead his horse in, for he dreaded the helplessness of being afoot.

His felt boots made no sound. As he hurried past the servants' quarters and down a hallway, he heard voices, in front: a challenge as of a drowsy porter, then brusque answer, and a scuffle which ended in a groan.

There was time. He hurried back, mounted up, and again felt complete. He nudged the stallion with his boot, and stroked the sleek neck, wheedling the bewildered beast into the tiled passageway.

A woman cried out, more in wrath and indignation than in fright. "Father of pigs! Get out of here or I will have you skinned alive."

"That's her, Olajai Turcan Aga!"

"Come down, *khanoum*; we won't hurt you."

"So you *do* know that this is Timur's house. You know, and come in?"

They laughed at the threat. "And we know where Timur is."

That was when the lame rider's scowl became a grin. "Come down, Olajai!" he called. "We're leaving town!"

The deep-chested hail made the men at arms whirl about. They had curved swords, they had maces; they wore peaked helmets, and armor of overlapping plates sewed on leather, but they were afoot, and they were surprised.

The stallion snorted. He quivered, then leaped as Timur's legs tightened. The heavy blade licked out, finding the gap between neck-guard and hauberk. As the stroke bit home, Timur traversed, so that the wall covered his left. He swayed in the saddle; a spike-headed "morning star" ripped his tunic, exposing the link mail beneath, and then his blade flickered, slashing the man's forehead.

Blood blinded; that one was out of action.

"Come down; we're riding!" Timur shouted.

Some were scrambling now to get to the front court, and their waiting horses; several tried to close in with swords. Blades clanged. Timur hewed down, slicing off plates of armor.

Olajai snatched a tall Chinese vase from the landing and heaved it on the head of the rearmost. While his helmet saved him from a smashed skull, the impact dropped him in his tracks. She dashed down the stairs, and plucked the fellow's helmet from his head.

"Put it on!" she cried, crowding up on Timur's left.

"Grab a horse!" he answered, and booted the stallion after the handful who had raced for their mounts.

And when his horse got firm footing on the hard-packed earth, Timur charged with effect.

Olajai followed. She was not dressed for riding, but the ripping of her gown took care of that. And she picked a good mount.

Two of the raiders galloped across the square. Two others fled afoot. Timur snatched the bow whose case hung from the saddle of Olajai's horse. As he strung it, she passed him an arrow.

The hindmost of the footmen pitched on his face.

Timur grinned. "Good bow. Now keep behind me; there'll be the devil to pay at the gate."

There was, but it did not last long.

Guardsmen were turning out. The two surviving horsemen had attended to that. But the moon was bright, and Timur's bowstring twanged, once, twice, thrice: the deadly Turki arrows, released at a dead run, cleared a path. Then a whirl of steel, and the fugitives went pelting down one of the lanes which threaded the orchard girdle of Samarkand.

CHAPTER II
THE BEGGAR

Once a bend in the lane furnished momentary cover, Timur pulled up. "Get Eltchi Bahadur and as many others as you can, and ride direct for Saghej Well. I'll keep the Kipchaks off your heels, and I'll meet you later."

Olajai had long since learned to think quickly, and to move while thinking; she waved, reined her horse down a cross lane, and galloped to notify the chief of Timur's fifty picked fighting men who had followed him from his home in Kesh. And since they lived outside the city walls, Olajai's task was safe enough.

Her brother, Mir Hussein, was at Saghej Well with forty odd retainers. They had outraced the Kipchaks to find refuge in the wastelands, and their heads apparently were not considered worth the cost in horseflesh.

Timur dismounted. When he heard the approach of the pursuers, he pretended to be picking a stone from his horse's hoof. In a moment they came into view, and in the full moon, they saw him. Olajai could not be far away. The horsemen reined in. It was over, they thought.

The fugitive, having the advantage of the moon, fired from his own shadow. A man toppled. Timur swung into the saddle, and the Ferghana stallion took off in a falcon swoop.

He twisted, shooting as he rode. And this was not his second choice horse!

They would stick. Speed was not the essence of this chase, since he had neither rations nor water nor a spare mount. As he gained a lead, he reined in a little, holding the distance just beyond arrow range. For all they knew, Olajai was ahead of him, just beyond sight.

Timur now had time to ponder on the reasons behind the raid on his house. Bikijek's resentment at a man who spent too much time blocking the sale of justice, blocking the extortion of doubled taxes, and the making of false returns: that was one fair guess. The other, plain court jealousy. Though the attempt to kidnap Olajai suggested a third answer—a blow at her exiled brother, or a stranglehold on Timur himself.

And as he rode, his memory reached back to that night when he had drunk his guests off their feet; it all came back, that survey at sunrise, of his littered banquet room.

He recalled the drums which had rolled and thundered across the broad median. They blotted out the muezzin's call to prayer. From a high window he could see the horsetail standards at Bikijek's door. The puppet king, Elias Koja, old Togluk Khan's son, let Bikijek play with the tokens of royalty, instead of setting to work with a running noose.

It would not, it could not last long, and when it ended, the Golden Horde of the Kipchak would restore order.

Order; herds eaten by Kipchak soldiers, granaries emptied by Kipchak officers, towns and farmsteads burned, and all Timur's broad acres in Kesh devastated with the rest. All because Bikijek, chief lord of the young king's court, had drums beaten five times daily before his palace.

Ten or a dozen local emirs, so busy battling each other that they had not stopped Elias Koja when his father sent him south to be Grand Khan of the Jagatai; that was the trouble. Rugged individualists, every man a king, and so now they had the Horde on their necks, and now their lands were the proving ground of an apprentice whose father had handed him the entire Jagatai heritage in which to learn the trade of kingship.

Timur had laughed aloud, for wine and fermented mare's milk had made him see the truth with a bitter clarity which his sober and busy days had never permitted. "First I fought Uncle Hadji, after Uncle Hadji and I drove Beyan Selduz out of town. Then they murdered Uncle Hadji, and I got an army to avenge him, and then the army divided into three parts and we had a war to settle the dividing of the booty. Every man a king. Allah! What we need is one king, and that one home grown. Too bad Mir Hussein's grandfather isn't alive."

He had smiled, in half drunken grimness and regret, thinking of the King Maker and the King Maker's grandson, handsome, hard fighting, Mir Hussein, fickle, crackbrained, unpredictable Hussein who had the loveliest sister in the world.

"Allah curse Bikijek, Allah curse every man who does not curse Bikijek's religion and his father and his grandfather!"

He had spoken aloud. A grave voice had made him turn. There, in the arched doorway stood a ragged man with a snarled beard; the slanting rays kept his face from being any too clear.

"Who asks Allah to curse the religion of another true believer?"

Timur snorted. "I'm talking to myself. Only way to do, if you want to hear sense for a change."

Then his eyes became used to the glare: he saw the grimy khelat, the greasy skullcap, the girdle of frayed rope, the dirty hands which fingered a wooden bowl. Dirty hands, this beggar had, but fine and long, made for good penmanship. And he wore a writing case at his girdle and a scroll carefully wrapped in a clean red silk scarf.

'Well, darvish!' Timur found a gold piece. "Guest of Allah, and a lot more welcome than these Kipchak pigs!"

Only then had his eyes a chance to focus sharply on the seamed face, shrewd, ironic, kindly; somewhat of a dish face, with broad, flat nose, Mongol features and melon head like Timur's own.

And Timur knelt on the littered tiles, catching the beggar's hand, too swiftly for any evasion; he kissed it.

"By the Splendor! I'd heard—I didn't recognize—"

The darvish freed his hand, made a gesture to decline the reverence "Kaboul Shah Aglen, now the Guest of God and the least of the slaves." Timur Bek had risen, to step back, entirely bewildered. Kaboul Shah Aglen, eighth in direct descent from Genghis Khan's son, Jagatai, begging his bread, and for shoes, growing calluses on his feet!

Kaboul smiled, "The darvish robe would fit you, Timur Bek. Last night's friends are this day's enemies. Become intoxicated by the splendor of Allah, and become His Guest, and the peace will be with you."

Outside, just then, horses had begun to squeal and snort; saddle drums rolled, for Bikijek was riding to the mosque. As the lordly sounds died out, Kaboul Aglen went on, "When Togluk Khan comes south to cure the disease which his son ignores, your palace becomes a mirage, and you'll be stealing sheep again. Get out, while you still can leave without killing too many horses.

"Genghis Khan, the master of all mankind, once had to steal a horse to keep from wearing out his boots. In me, the circle closes on itself. I beg my bread, as in the end all the race of Genghis Khan must do."

Timur's face darkened; Karashar Nevian, his ancestor, nine generations back had been Genghis Khan's uncle and advisor. Then he laughed, and it was like trumpets braying before the charge. "See here! You're the heir to the Jagatai throne, you, not Togluk Khan nor Togluk Khan's son. I'll make you Grand Khan in Samarkand!"

The beggar shrugged. "No time; too soon, you'll be riding for your neck. You, not Bikijek."

Timur flipped the golden dinar into the bowl.

The beggar whisked it out. "What is nothing now will be your fortune soon, and the peace upon you!"

And here it was: hard riding pursuit behind him, while his wife raced to round up what fighting men she could find. So he laughed again, from thinking on the words of Kaboul Aglen, and the murderous bowstring a scribe could pluck.

Forty-two horsemen, all with spare mounts, waited with Olajai when two days later, Timur's horse stumbled toward the rendezvous, where tents were scattered about a spring which kept the grass green,

Hashim, melon headed and scar-faced, came

running to greet him; and he walked back, clinging to Timur's stirrup leather. "We ride again, tura!" he said, using the Turki word for "my lord." "It is like the old days again."

Then Timur saw Tagi Bouga Barlas, his distant cousin, hard bitten and grinning; Sayfuddin, the greatest archer of them all, coddling a bow; and roaring Elthci Bahadur whose strength and skill had thus far hacked his way out of all the traps into which he charged. They crowded about, grimy and sweat gleaming; jeweled collars and gold inlaid helmets and embroidered belts grotesque against greasy khalats, and sheepskin jackets.

"*Hai*, Timur Bahadur!"

Quickly they broke camp and rode, for they had rested while Timur led the Kipchak riders a crazy chase in circles. And now, being among friends, Timur dozed in the saddle; and Olajai rode beside him.

CHAPTER III
BATTLE

Five days brought Timur to the Jihun's poplar lined banks; and swimming this river put the Jagatai realm behind them. At the Well of Saghej they found Mir Hussein, with Dilshad Aga, his wife, and some forty horsemen.

The King Maker's grandson was handsome as his sister was lovely; a small, pointed black beard, and high arched brows, and a high bridged, straight nose with nostrils whose flare made one think of a stallion scenting a fight. Until his army had been scattered, he had been King in Kandahar; now he had lost everything but hope.

There was no meat, so they ate cooked millet and buttered tea. Mir Hussein said, "*Bismillahi*, it could be worse."

Timur grimaced. "We can't eat sand very long. But with a couple good raids, I'll have an army at my back. The men of Kesh were giving me hard looks, you'd think I'd sold them out, just because I took the thankless job of trying to stand between them and those Kipchak hounds! But this fast ride has set a lot of them thinking."

"*Inshallah!* But I can't show up in Kandahar with a guard of forty men."

Timur chuckled sourly. "No, they've probably got a new king there. That's the trouble, too many kings, instead of one good one. Now, your grandfather—"

Mir Hussein sighed. "May God be well pleased with him! But do you think he could improve things? He used to pull kings out of his saddlebags, but this is different. Still, you'd do pretty well as Grand Khan of the Jagatai."

Dangerous ground. If Timur did raise an army to drive the present puppet out of Samarkand, he'd be quite a hero, but once he took the throne, jealousy would start feud. Mir Hussein was good in battle, and good nowhere else. "You're the grandson of Mir Kazagan," Timur countered. "How's Tekil?"

"Hungry and looking for business. At least seven hundred Turkomans and the like."

"Our hundred will draw his following," Timur argued. "And with that start, we'll begin to make an impression."

So they rode through the march of hell, across the black sands of Kivac. The scrawny oasis looked like a small paradise, for the lips Timur's men were cracked from thirst.

The citadel loomed up, above the poplars. "I don't like it," Timur said. "No one working in the fields. No one tending the ditches."

Instead of pressing on to the city, they made camp at the fringe of green which marked the beginning of cultivation.

Timur beckoned to Eltchi Bahadur and Tagai Bouga Barlas. "We'll ride in and pay our respects to Tekil."

Hussein cut in, "No! Let me go. He knows I've spent a couple of months at the Well of Saghej, and he made no trouble. Let me talk to him."

Timur's eyes narrowed. "Hmmm . . . don't tell him I'm here. Just say you know where I am."

The deep-set Turki eyes sparkled. "So you've been thinking about that mess in Samarkand?"

Where Hussein had been the ill favored one, it now seemed that Timur's head was most in demand.

That night, Timur posted double guards and slept with his boots on. While his fame as a captain would always get him followers, it would also make his head a prize in a land where every man was a king, and allegiances changed overnight.

In the morning he heard trumpets and drums, and saw Mir Hussein's standard, and the riders who came from the gates, the fields and through the groves.

"Break camp, and be ready to mount up!" Timur commanded.

Then he rode out with twenty men to meet Tekil.

Ceremonious greetings: the burly governor fairly fell from his horse to be the first to dismount. A big, red-faced man, a hearty, smiling man. "Welcome, welcome, Timur Bek! Kivak is yours. You and your brother, I bid you welcome."

Tekil had an escort of perhaps two hundred horses. Timur wondered where the others were. He caught old Hashim's narrowed eyes, and made a twist of head and chin. The old fellow gave a gesture of assent; and unobtrusively edged from the clump of horsemen, to head back to camp.

More compliments. Hussein was smooth and smiling and affable. Tomorrow, he and Timur would with pleasure and heartiness attend the governor's banquet. Today, Allah bear witness, things were in an uproar in camp. Horses, badly overtaxed, needed attention. And some of the party was still unaccounted for. *Ay, Wallah!* Some baggage animals, carrying all the gifts designed for His Excellency, were lagging a day's march behind.

Something was wrong, something was off color; Hussein's fluent patter confirmed Timur's earlier premonitions. He said, cutting in brusquely, "Allied-to-Greatness, we beg permission to turn from the light of your Presence!"

Words and music did not matter. He was in the saddle before Tekil fairly realized that another speaker had addressed him. Tagi Bouga Barlas mounted up; and so did Hussein.

Tekil's face changed. And then came the great bawling voice of Eltchi Bahadur, and the pounding of hooves. "To horse, O Bek! The bastard's got us hemmed in!"

"Swords out!"

And Timur had scarcely shouted his command when an arrow smacked home with a solid thump. Eltchi was shooting, shooting hard, fast, straight. "Get out of my way," he howled, "get out of my way!"

Timur and Mir Hussein were blocking his line of fire. Then the visitors and the host's men went into action, blades out; some lancers maneuvered for working space, while others threw their lances down and snatched maces from their saddle bows.

"To camp!" Timur shouted. "Archers fall out!"

There was no drill by command, as such; it was rather instinctive teamwork, based on many a pitched battle and running fight. Eltchi Bahadur charged headlong at the Tekil's guard. Hacking and hewing, he was swallowed up by milling horsemen and billowing dust.

Meanwhile, as though called by signal, half Timur's escort swooped to right and left, and the bows began to twang. Hard driven shafts laced the flanks of Tekil's tight packed traitors; murderous, close range archery; cunningly driven shafts, some picking men, others nailing horses whose fall would block the movement of other riders.

Stung by the ferocious archery, Tekil's men opened out. Timur and Hussein pressed in, head on, to divide the enemy. And from the rear came the brawling, booming voice of Eltchi Bahadur. He looked as though an avalanche had passed over him, but he was hewing his way back to meet Timur.

Timur's archers fell back, shooting as they withdrew and covering the retreat. Over the roar of battle, he heard the approach of his main detachment, and saw his chance. "This way, you bawling bull!" he shouted to Eltchi, and pointed toward a low hillock.

In a moment, Timur's standard was on the knoll.

Dust ringed the oasis. The rest of Tekil's men were closing in. It was now clear where the governor's force had been. It was all too clear that the riders trailing Timur out of Samarkand had been baiting him, while a courier rode directly to Tekil. Bikijek, he now concluded, had known all the while where Mir Hussein was, and had counted on Timur's joining his brother-in-law: the two were to be settled beyond the border of the Jagatai territory.

Ten to one: Timur took a fresh horse, and looked out and down at the closing circle of steel. He said to his wife, and to Dilshad Aga, "Keep your heads down. There won't be many of us to block the arrows, not for long."

CHAPTER IV
OLAJAI

The one sided battle was reaching its end as the sun slowly dragged down toward the horizon. Olajai, ignoring arrows, went about during lulls, carrying a goatskin jar of brackish water.

"Easier each round," Timur said, and licked the dust from his lips.

She laughed. "They're well whittled down, too!"

Of Tekil's men, scarcely fifty were able to fight: the others were dead, or they had left the field because of wounds. As for Timur, only seven were about his standard.

Charge after charge had been swept back, for in the beginning, Tekil's men had blocked each other, only a few at a time being able to present themselves to the enemy; and closing in on Eltchi Bahadur was a swift way to the mercy of Allah.

Those who first charged up the little knoll had struggled in sandy soil, facing a hail of arrows: and the next wave had been blocked by windrows of fallen horses and men. Finally, exhaustion took the heart from all but the strongest. Skill failed, and so did the will.

"Only seven to one now, my dear! Give Bahadur a drink!"

He turned to his sister-in-law: "I'll get you horse tails, tie them to the standard."

There were plenty of once splendid mounts who had no further use for their tails. Timur hacked, and Dilshad Aga set to work.

Timur waited. The ring of winded, wounded enemies waited. The air had the dead stillness of a well-fired oven, except when hot wind drove scorching sand. Tagi Bouga Barlas and Sayfuddin were now on foot. Eltchi Bahadur grinned, though wearily; blood and sweat and dust made his homely face a devil's mask.

"Hai, Bahadur! The sons of pigs would turn tail if someone knocked that Tekil out of action."

Timur snorted. "I've spent all day trying to get at him. I've been cutting meat till my arm's ready to fall off, he always gets someone between me and him."

Hussein came up; debonair, head cocked like the head of a falcon, eyes aglitter. "Why take down our standard, brother?"

"It's coming up in a second." Then Dilshad Aga called, and Timur went to take the staff. Hussein saw the three horse tails. "The standard of Genghis Khan! By Allah, why not? This is our day. God does what he will do, and here we are."

Timur planted the staff, and said to Hashim, "Sound off!"

The one unbroken saddle drum rolled and grumbled in the hot silence; a hot wind made the three horse tails ripple, then fan out. Timur challenged the enemy: "Sons of Bad Mothers! Here is the standard of Genghis Khan, the Master of all Mankind. He rides again!"

Hussein mounted up, wordlessly, and with the smooth swiftness of a panther. Sword out, he raced down the slope. Then came Eltchi Bahadur's great voice; the drum stopped rumbling. Olajai cried out— many men had died, but this was her brother, and a clump of swordsmen had swallowed him up.

The others were at his heels. Tekil's standard, clipped in half, was trampled in the dust. Eltchi Bahadur smashed home with all his weight and steel. And as he raced, Timur plucked his bow. One shot. Just one. A single shaft, threading through the shifting fighters, caught Tekil between the teeth. The impact knocked him from his horse.

Then an arrow caught Timur's mount. The beast crumpled, flinging the rider asprawl. Timur rolled, recovered, and from the bloody sand he snatched a half-pike. Eltchi Bahadur had hewn a path to Tekil. Timur bore down on the pike, driving through armor, driving it through the man, and deep into the earth.

Whoever could run or ride fled to the fortress. Seven wounded victors left the field, to find whatever safety they could, before Tekil's men recovered from the shock, and began to think of vengeance.

They retraced their course. At the desert's fringe, three of the survivors said, "Lord Timur, Allah does what he will do, and with your permission, we go to our homes in Khorassan, while you raise an army."

This also had happened before, so Timur answered, "Go with my blessing."

Then on the night when they were not far from the Jihun, Timur said to Hussein, "There are not enough for any defense, only enough to be conspicuous. Better we separate. You go to Hirmen, and spend the winter with the Mikouzeri tribesmen. I'll go back home to Kesh, incognito, and I'll meet you in Hirmen, later."

So they parted. And when Timur was alone with Olajai, he said, "*Shireen*, you married a prince in Kesh, and now look! Not one rider behind me."

"I'm not worrying. Though I was scared silly, until you had that crazy notion of hoisting three horse tails!"

He eyed her sharply. "You quit worrying then? Mmmm . . . it did something to your brother, the crackbrain, he was off before I knew what was happening."

She nodded. "That shocked me, too. Then, suddenly, I knew that Tekil's men would break. For a crazy instant, it was as if Genghis Khan had come back through all these nine generations, and out of his grave."

"The sun, my dear. It was bad."

She shook her head. "I didn't see anything, I didn't hear anything, I just felt something. As though you had really had the right, that moment, to put up the horse tail standard. And they felt it."

"You're giving Eltchi Bahadur and Hussein not much credit!"

"I notice you took the tails off before we left. I'm not worried. It's working out. What that darvish said. Only he didn't say *all*. Maybe he didn't know, maybe he couldn't see so far ahead. But I do."

"What's that?" His voice was sharp.

"My grandfather made kings. He unmade them. Always, he put on the throne of Samarkand someone of the direct line of Genghis Khan. And there was peace, the very name made peace. You know, he could have taken the throne himself."

"He could. And Kazagan Khan would have filled any throne."

"But he didn't, he wouldn't. Timur—don't you see what I mean? You have a right to the name, you've proved the right, back there."

They marched, from brackish well to drywell where there was water only by digging. Then the worst of the two horses collapsed. Timur dismounted and said "Take mine."

She gaped. He said gruffly, "Mount up!"

"Why —darling—whatever—you're crazy."

Her incredulity was natural. A man tramping on foot would be too worn out to fight. It was plain sense that he should ride while Olajai walked.

"But—"

"Mount up!" he commanded and she obeyed.

He tramped along holding the stirrup leather.

And that afternoon toward sunset as they halted to rest he looked at his boots. The soles were gone.

"See! The darvish is right! Timur of the race of Genghis Khan is barefooted. This thing had to be. And now that I cannot go any lower I must go higher and the Power is with God!"

She was no longer worried by his seeming madness in walking while a woman rode. "You lied to me, you knew what happened on that knoll, as well as I did!"

They were coming near to a well, or to where one should be. The sun's level rays bent into their backs so that their shadows reached long and dark ahead of them.

Then he saw the horsemen riding into the glare. "How many?" he asked Olajai, very calmly.

"Ten—twelve—fifteen—too many, Timur, and you've been walking."

"Who are they—what are they?"

"Turkomans," she answered. "I was afraid of that." The Governor of Kivac's force had been largely Turkoman.

Olajai said, lightly, "We can't use horse tails again. We haven't enough horses."

She started to slide out of the saddle, so that he could mount up. He said, "Not yet. The glare keeps them from seeing that there are two of us."

When they reached the well, and its thin cover of scrawny trees, he made the horse turn, so that it screened the next move. Olajai slid from the saddle. He took his lariat and secured it to a root which reached from the wall of the well.

"It's dry. The water is in the other hole. Get down and stay down. You're near enough now to get to the river afoot."

Then he mounted up, drew his sword, and rode at them, shouting his challenge. He had no more arrows. The riders had fanned out to envelop the oasis, so as to block the escape of any other travelers who might be there. Every sign pointed to being cut down and robbed of his arms, his horse gear, the jewels of his belt and scabbard; so he shouted, "Timur, the Man of Kesh, Timur, the son of Tragai!"

A man cried an answer. The archers lowered their bows. That one man rode forward and dismounted.

"Timur Bek! Welcome, and the blessing of Allah, and the Peace of Allah upon you! We heard that you had gone this way, and we came to meet you."

So Olajai came from the pit. Timur gave her bracelets to Hadji Mehemmed, the Turkoman raider with whom he had ridden once, some years previous. And Hadji Mehemmed gave them horses, and an escort of ten men. Olajai said, that night, "This proves it—the horse tails are still with you."

CHAPTER V
"SPREAD THE GOOD WORD"

At Bokar-Zendin, Timur left Olajai with friends, for being north of the Jihun again, he risked recognition, ambush, betrayal, which he would not have Olajai share. "More than that," he said, "if you went, I'd be recognized just that much sooner."

"Women's chatter? Well, men haven't done too well by you!"

Timur chuckled amiably at that painfully just quip. "*Shireen*, wherever we were guests, and we couldn't always refuse hospitality without making ourselves even more conspicuous, there'd be women

looking at you. They'd guess, and much sooner than any men would, looking at us."

"Mmmm . . . yes, of course."

Now that the blame had been passed to superior feminine perception, Olajai felt better about it all. So the Lord of Kesh sneaked thief-like across the lands of his ancestors, not even daring to enter his own estate, for this choice territory was packed with Kipchaks.

A lone archer limped through the market place. Timur, being afoot, had the best possible disguise, yet the risk was deadly enough, since men of Bikijek's clique came in from Samarkand every day.

One by one, he cornered retainers who had ridden with his late father, Emir Tragai. These had to look twice before they could believe that this haggard footman was Timur Bek. Each one said. "Lord Timur, we thought that you had quit us. We were glad when we heard that you'd left Samarkand with a troop on your heels. Then we knew that you were with us in heart, and in the end, you would come back and wipe them out."

"What with?"

"We join whatever army you raise."

Close-mouthed, weather-beaten men listened to him and then spread the word. When he left Kesh, Temouka Kutchin rode after him with twenty horsemen ready for the field.

They took the trail for Badakshan. The story of his desperate fight against Tekil of Kivac had spread, and one chieftain after another joined him. There was Bahram Jalair, and a distant cousin, Saddik Barlas; Kazanchi Hassan with a hundred horse came seeking him. Mir Sayfuddin, whom he had not seen since the disaster in the desert, had meanwhile raised seventy picked men. Another kinsman, Koja Barlas, had a like party. Then came Shir Bahrain, and Ulum Kuli with two hundred horse, Mamut Keli with as many footmen.

Timur's disaster and his barefooted march across the desert recruited more men more easily than any success had ever done.

Even the Kipchak Horde helped him: for with Bikijek's nobles now leading raiding parties over all the Jagatai territory, captain after captain fled to join Timur.

When he met Mir Hussein and they reviewed their combined forces, Timur said, "Now that the enemy has taught them that too much freedom is no freedom at all, they've stopped being kings."

Spies came, saying that the Kipchak raids were becoming more severe. Worse yet, Togluc Khan had sent some 20,000 of the Golden Horde to the north, to reinforce his son, Elias Koja.

"We're not ready. What we have is good, by Allah,

but not enough. Time is against us," Hussein said.

"Time is the toy of Allah," Timur retorted. "He does with it what pleases Him."

"It pleased Him to have most of us wiped out facing odds of ten to one," Hussein pointed out, realistically.

And these men would follow Timur only as long as they willed, and no longer. Even Genghis Khan, more nearly an absolute lord than any man who had ever ruled men, had ruled only by the will of his captains: Asiatic democracy, masquerading as a despotism.

So Timur's frown deepened, and even more when he heard that Kesh was heavily garrisoned. Worst of all, spies said that Olajai, finally leaving Bokar-Zendan to him and her brother, had been recognized and trapped; she was a captive in Kesh, a hostage for his good behavior,

Timur asked the messenger, "Who else has heard this?"

"No one, *tura*, save yourself and Mir Hussein."

"I'll take your head," Timur solemnly swore, "I'll skin you and stuff your hide with straw if a word of it leaks out in camp. Is that clear?"

"Aywah, tura."

He gave the man a handful of golden *dinars*, and dismissed him.

Then, to Hussein: "I've got to get her out of there."

"I take refuge with Allah! My own sister, but you can risk a good little army against a walled city, just for a woman? Timur, that's not sense. Your men'll think you're crazy, wasting them on a woman."

Timur smiled. "That's something I'm not telling them."

"Allah! But what?"

"Listen."

The drums sounded assembly, and the trumpets brayed. Timur spoke from the saddle: "O Men! Friends of my father and my uncle, a saint came to me in a dream last night. Allah has promised us our city. Even though we had green boughs instead of lances, our faith would make us win.

"The Presence of Genghis Khan came into the desert, and our enemies ran.

"And if we take Kesh, every captain from Badakshan to Kandahar will join us to share in our next glory. When they join, who will stop us?"

He sold them as they stood there. And not even on the march, the hard forced march on Kesh, did a man of them wonder what Timur would do for siege engines.

"They're drunk," Hussein said. "Drunk and not from wine. How did you do it?"

"I don't know. It came to me."

"Well, if we do capture Kesh," Hussein countered, "they'll besiege us, and have you ever seen a Mongol or Turk who was any good, locked up behind walls?"

Timur laughed triumphantly. "Hai! Out of your own mouth, brother! The very truth that's going to make Kesh open up in no time. Go and spread the word! Keep them with a dream in their eyes!"

They rode so fast that there was no news of their coming.

Bivouac: and at dawn, far off, rose the gray walls of Kesh, high above the orchards.

"Now get busy," Timur said to his captains. "Cut off green boughs. Divide into four columns." He saw their faces change at this insane suggestion, but he gave them no chance to object. "Let each column mark the time, and do it in this wise—"

They listened, they grinned, their slanted eyes widened, and then they howled and drew their swords to hew limbs from the forest.

Timur with a picked handful emerged from the woods, and raced down into the plain, and toward the fields. He had all the musicians: and all were sounding off brazen trumpets and saddle drums and ear-slashing cymbals. Musicians on horse, musicians on camel back, and a picked troop of lancers: they moved at the pace of a polo game, Kipchak guards came from Kesh to welcome what they believed to be fellow invaders.

"Swords out!"

Though not caught entirely off guard, they might as well have been. They were cut down, and their horses galloped wildly home with empty saddles: and Timur resumed his bold race.

By now the gates of Kesh were closed. When Timur reined in, his archers shadowed him with a curtain of arrows. He demanded, "Surrender at once, and we'll let you march out alive."

A man in heavy Khorassan mail risked his head. Timur's archers ceased firing. The garrison commander came up to the parapet. The man was puzzled: a hundred horse seemed hardly the right force to take a walled town.

"You're crazy!" he raged. "Or drunk. Who are you?"

"Timur Bek, and what are you doing in my town?"

The bold challenge took the commander aback. "I am Daulat Ali, and I hold this in the name of Elias Koja, Khan of Samarkand, Son of Togluk Khan."

"You can become wealthy and famous by taking my head," Timur reminded him "Bikijek wants it badly."

Daulat Ali was no drill ground soldier; Bikijek didn't send that kind out to hold a town. Yet he was worried. There must be a sizable army on the way, and there had been no warning.

Timur went on. "March your garrison out. One hour's delay, and I'll have the head of every fifth man, taken by count, with no regard to rank."

"You can't take a town with that handful!" Daulat Ali retorted.

"Only Allah knows what is in my hand! Trifle a bit longer, and not one of you leaves alive. Quick, man! You're up on the wall. Look around. Do you want a siege, or do you think you'd like to try a sortie?"

On the four horizons, great columns of dust rose. Each was drawing toward Kesh. Citizens were now on the walls, some of Timur's own people. They began to yell, "Allah! Armies from Khorassan! Armies from Kabul!"

Rioting broke out within the town. Timur grinned when he heard the shouting. "I won't have to take your heads, they'll tend to that before I can save you fellows!"

Heaving water jugs and roofing tiles from housetops may annoy soldiers, but such civilian resistance rarely gets far. That was what worried Daulat Ali. Timur must have promised his people four armies, or they'd never be crazy enough to stone Kipchak hard cases.

Timur could now see the dust columns from the ground level. "If you move fast enough you'll have a chance to warn the apprentice king."

Turning the garrison loose, instead of taking them prisoner or cutting them down would give Elias Koja and Bikijek a nasty shock. Only a strong army could afford such a gesture of contempt. And Daulat Ali, already shaken, signaled to his trumpeters; they sounded recall.

The disarmed garrison filed out, and rapidly enough not to see that they had surrendered to dust clouds raised by horsemen dragging green branches.

And when Timur found Olajai, he said, "Home again, shireen, but only Allah knows how long we'll stay."

CHAPTER VI
KING-MAKER

By the time his spies had caught up with him, Timur realized that though he would quickly have to abandon Kesh he had at least succeeded in more than a personal enterprise: his daring capture of the city was bringing hundreds of one-time doubters to his standard.

And then Timur learned that Elias Koja's army, strongly reinforced by his father's troops, had moved out of Samarkand. They were going toward the Jihun, to make a clean sweep of the Jagatai lands and possibly to invade Khorassan.

So Timur and his newly won recruits got out of Kesh before Elias Koja's general, Bikijek, could learn that green branches had swept his garrison out of town.

Timur won the bridge with a few hours to spare. Then from the Khorassan side, he saw *touman* after *touman* of Kipchak troops, each 10,000 strong. The apprentice king's father was out for conquest. "Brother." Mir Hussein said, "our army will scatter like dust, once we start running. They'll forget that trick at Kesh."

"Then we won't run."

"We can't face 60,000 Kipchaks, not when Bikijek leads them."

Olajai came from behind the red carpet which, hanging from its long fringes, separated her quarters from the reception room of the pavilion. "Remember the horse tails, Timur!" she cut in.

Hussein turned on his sister. "You little fool, how long will Allah's patience last! Bluffing Bikijek is not quite the same as scaring a blockhead out of Kesh!"

Timur scowled. "I've got an army. One retreat, and they'll go back to their sheep."

"Yes, and just one bout with the Golden Horde, and they'll be minced mutton. You can't keep on recruiting on the strength of glorious defeats like the one at Kivak!"

"The horse tails," Olojai repeated. "The Presence!"

Timur rose. "We can hold the bridge for a day."

So he went to dispose his six thousand against ten times as many.

From sunrise to sunset, troop after troop of Kipchaks charged the bridgehead, taking their toll, but going down before the stubborn defense. Timur and Eltchi Bahadur plied mace and sword; and the sight and sound of them steadied the little army. Yet when the sun sank, they were tired and battered: wearied from the very cutting down of successive waves.

That night, spies swam the Jihun. In speech and dress and face, they matched the enemy; and they could mix freely, grumbling about the stiff resistance, and muttering about Timur's reserves, spread out, well behind the Jihun. And they muttered about the fall of Kesh. . . .

Meanwhile, Timur was moving, He left only five hundred to hold the bridge: which picked men could do, for another day. The others divided, half going upstream, half downstream, well beyond hearing of the enemy, to risk the dangerous fords.

Bikijek could have made a similar attempt, but with his overwhelming force, it seemed far more sensible to hammer for another day, and drive through the troops who held the bridge.

Finally, there was the rumor of Timur's reserves; Bikijek was too good a general to risk being cut up in such fashion. Once he learned—

But Bikijek had no chance to learn.

Timur's losses by drowning were smaller than they could have been, had he and his captains not known every foot of the treacherous fords. Time and again, he went back, each time with a fresh horse, to lead the next detachment over. And on the final trip, he listened to a spy just returned: "Togluk Khan is dead! His son was about to go home when there was news of us."

Timur turned to Hussein, who commanded the final party.

"Allah is with us! There is a fear in Elias Koja. When he should go to Kipchak to receive the allegiance of his father's lords, and take the old man's throne, he stays here. The raid on Kesh has shaken him!"

Timur led his *hazaras* into the hills well behind the Kipchak camp. He spread them far apart. "Make fires," he commanded. "Many fires. As of many bivouacked *toumans*."

That night, he looked down on the fires of Bikijek's six *toumans*. And that night, Bikijek looked backward and upward at fires which suggested a force at least equal to his own: and a force which had slipped up between him, and Samarkand, and the long trail to Kipchak.

At dawn, with all his men carefully under cover in the woods at the foot of the slope, Timur watched Bikijek's scouts patrolling the river. The Kipchaks were worried; they had not resumed the attack on the bridgehead. Fires behind them at night, and now, they found hoof prints at the dangerous fords. As they saw it, Timur, with far more army than anyone had credited him with having, had held the bridge in order to make a night crossing to cut off their retreat, and so drive them into the river,

Bikijek's troops were soon in motion. First, they were going to withdraw; second, they were going to make the best disposition after what they considered a thorough outmaneuvering.

Then came Timur's charge: not from the distant line of the past night's campfires, but from the forest at the foot of the hills. Either too early, or too late, it could not have succeeded, despite the advantage of surprise; but Timur's lightning slash was timed to the second. He caught the Kipchaks when they were neither set for defense, nor fully committed to withdrawal.

Some tried to rush the bridge. Other *hazaras* fled along the bank. Those who tried to reform and fight it out were blocked by disorganized units. And Timur's troops picked the heart of the opposition: Bikijek's *touman*, and the force led by Tokatmur.

Elias Koja's standard went down before the rush. Tokatmur, second in command to Bikijek, fell under the fury of swords which followed the final flight of arrows. And it was like the moves of a chess game long reasoned out in advance: one-two-three, and checkmate.

The apprentice king escaped, and so did Bikijek, one leaving behind him a throne, the other losing an army. And when the trumpets sounded recall from cutting down the fugitives, Timur formed his troops and raced on to Samarkand.

As he rode back through the city from which he and Olajai had so narrowly escaped, the citizens who crowded the streets and packed the housetops, began to shout, "*Sahib Karan!* Lord of the Age!"

He had conquered a city by dust, and he had triumphed over an army by fire: and Olajai said, "When the Jagatai princes meet they'll make you Grand Khan of Samarkand."

She was right. Hussein had said as much; and the Barlas clan, Timur's uncle's kinsmen, were behind him. But as he rode toward the palace vacated forever by Elias Koja, Timur made plans of his own.

That night, serving men dragged monstrous trays into the banquet hall: camels roasted entire, and sheep; and there was horseflesh, and leather trays heaped with rice and millet. Others set out jars of wine, and jars of fermented mare's milk, and flagons that only a Mongol could drain.

Eltchi Bahadur was there, roaring as on the battlefield; Hussein, sleek and smooth and handsome as a panther; and the Barlas clan, flat-faced, grim and slant-eyed; Turki and Mongol in silken tunic and silken *khalat*. Though Togluk Khan the tyrant had died a natural death, horsemen still raced northward to deny his son any chance of an equally quiet end.

It was complete; complete, except for two things: Timur Bek was not present, and the grand *khan*'s dais at the head of the great hall was empty. Lords and captains, beks and emirs, ranged in rank on either side, with that one high place vacant: election day in Samarkand.

Some laughed. Some muttered. Ali sniffed the savor of roasted meat, and wine ready for the drinking. But Timur, *Sahib-Karan*, the Lord of the times, was late.

Then the drums rolled and the long trumpets brayed. Guards marched in, escorting a horse tail standard. In the courtyard soldiers shouted, "*Hai, Bahadur! Sahib Karan*, Timur, Grand Khan of Samarkand, Khan of the Jagatai!"

The uproar of the rank and file told the *emirs* and the beks how they had better vote; and they knew that wholesale desertions would follow an unpopular choice. Most of the Jagatai princes agreed with their men; but some scowled. For Timur to make a point of delaying his entry until all the others had arrived was laying it on too heavily; and for him to have the horse tail standard carried before him was taking too much for granted.

But the shouts from the court gave the lords no choice.

Then they saw who preceded Timur: a bearded man in the ragged robe of a darvish; a man who protested, a man who, though handled with respect, was being hustled into the hall, and toward the vacant high place.

At the foot of the dais, Timur halted with his barefooted companion. He raised his hand and the shouting ceased.

"O Men! In the days of your grandfathers, Kazagan Khan the Turk could have taken the throne of Samarkand but this he did not do; instead, he set up one of the blood of Genghis Khan, the Master of All Mankind, and used all his force to maintain one whom no one would deny or envy!

"Here is the darvish, here is the Guest of Allah, here is Kaboul Shah Aglen, directly descended from Genghis Khan's son Jagatai! Here is one who cares so little for power that he turns his back on thrones, and contemplates the splendor of Allah! Here is one with wisdom, not pride.

"Where we have each been kings, there has been no strength, and from too much freedom, we had an invader on our necks! So let this man be Grand Khan, for there is not one of us too proud to serve him!"

The shouting drowned the protests of the darvish. He could not deny his duty. They put an embroidered *khalat* over his ragged gown; they made him ascend the dais, and each prince in turn bowed nine times before him, as the ancient custom prescribed.

And when the banquet ended, the following noon, Timur Bek went to his own house, where Olajai waited.

"So you gave away a throne? After the Presence that came to you on the hill at Kivak?"

Timur was a little drunk, and he was tired, and he was hoarse from song and shouting. "He is the ninth generation, and all things go in nines with the race of Genghis Khan. Your brother and the others would soon turn against me—yet I can hold them together, serving him. And we won't have too many kings."

She looked up, smiling; her disappointment was gone. "The Presence will return to you, Timur." Then, just in the interests of discipline: "Allah, but you've slopped wine all over yourself, you're an awful looking mess for a King-Maker, you're as bad as my grandfather. You're ready to fall on your face!"

BLIND MAN'S BLUFF

by Edwin Baird

There be many kinds of critics—as many kinds, or nearly, as there are things to criticize.

To cite but a few, there is the sappy critic, the snappy critic, the youthful or cynical critic, the near or would-be critic, the critic who thinks witticism is criticism, the critic who thinks irascibility is original-ity, the critic who thinks a dysthetic body is an es-thetic mind, and the intuitive critic. And the best of these, I sometimes hold, is the intuitive critic.

By intuitive critic, I mean the critic who bases judgment not upon dry and hackneyed laws and tenets, nor upon friendship, nor upon enmity, but upon instinct, and instinct only. Such a critic—

But this is to be no dissertation on critics.

This is to be the story of the Kentucky Chicken Farm, the Girl with the Beautiful Brown Eyes, and the Desperate Young Artist.

I am—or was—the Desperate Young Artist.

Ask me not wherefore. I don't know, I'm sure. It wasn't my enemies; it may have been my friends; and I've often had a sneaking suspicion that my family was to blame. But I'm not sure.

At the sapient age of five or thereabouts I had an overwhelming ambition to be a brakeman on a freight-train; this quickly passed, and was followed by an intense longing to wear a bearskin cap and a red coat and twirl a baton thirty feet in the air at the head of a brass band.

At the age of fifteen I began to consider the advan-tages of being President. After exhaustive cogitation, I decided the pay did not merit the worry, and gave up thinking about it.

Then came the Great Passion.

I began to dabble in, with, and around art.

I believe I immortalized everything in the town, from the bantam rooster in our back yard to the pickle barrel in front of Jimson's Racket Store.

I decorated the front sitting room with my paint-ings, and friends of the family came and admired, and predicted great things for me, and I began to let my hair grow long and my trousers grow baggy—no true artist ever creases his trousers, of course—and affected flowing neckties, a velveteen jacket, and a hungry expression.

When I had begged, borrowed, earned, saved, and otherwise accumulated money enough, I took an art course in a correspondence school; and when I received my diploma, all nice and new in a pasteboard tube, I blacked my boots, donned my flowingest tie, packed an amplitudinous telescope, and with many tearful farewells and golden plaudits, accompanied by the whining of the family dog and the purring of the household cat, I left my dear old home in sunny Tennessee (a little quivering music, if you please, professor) and started out alone and unafraid to battle and conquer the cold, heartless world.

Let me say to you that when I boarded the train that morning for Chicago, Illinois, I was just as positive that some day the name of Jefferson Davis Mayfair would be as famous as the latest brand of chewing gum as I was that Jefferson Davis Mayfair was my name. There was never even a shadow of a mite of a scrap of a scintilla of a doubt about that.

Some persons have an idea that Chicago is a bad town for poets and painters and such. All a mistake.

Why, I could take you around Chicago tomorrow and point out to you any number of wielders of the brush who earn good wages embellishing West Madison Street with puffy jowled gents smoking five-cent cigars, or riders of Pegasus who fare equally well inditing triolets and roundelays to the meaty merits of Packingtown products. But, unfortunately, my ideals emphatically forbade this. I could not thus commercialize my art. In consequence, I would certainly have starved to death or gone to work had it not been for sundry letters from home containing words of good cheer and postal money-orders. I must admit that art flourished not well with me.

Shortly after my arrival in Chicago I rented a studio in the Parthenon Apartments on the North Side. There were many things I liked about the Parthenon, chief among them being its Bohemian atmosphere—whatever that is. There was no mistaking the atmosphere, however; it fairly reeked of garlic and turpentine and cheap, plug-cut tobacco.

Next to winning fame with my brush, palette, and tubes, I most desired a Bohemian atmosphere. I had often read of it in magazines, and heard of it from certain Tennesseans who had journeyed afar and seen strange things, and to at last be actually in it and of it was like having a dream come true.

On the other hand, there were annoying features about the Parthenon.

One was a hatefully ambitious pianist who lived and practiced directly opposite my studio window; nothing separated us but a ten-foot air-shaft, and into my ears was hammered at all hours sounds weird and harsh.

Another was the landlord's agent, who had an extremely unpleasant habit of demanding rent promptly when it was due. Both were bad.

Sometimes I would be soaring aloft on the wings of an inspiration, when—tap, tap, tap—and the agent's collector would be waiting without.

Anon, I would be moiling and sweating over my masterpiece, when—crash, bang! —and that terrible pianist would let fly his wildest.

I remember one dark, drizzling day in May.

I was in my studio, gazing ruefully at a painting I had expected to sell and hadn't, and fingering a lonesome piece of silver I thought was a quarter and wasn't, when came a tapping at my door, I knew it. It was the rent man's. I could always distinguish his odiously gentle tapping from other people's knocking.

Simultaneously with this dread tap, the frenzied pianist broke forth in all his fury.

Now, truly, this was piling Ossa on Pelion, and Lookout Mountain on top of both.

I got rid of the collector by jerking my hand from my pocket, showing him my— merciful Heavens! It was a nickel!—swearing it was all I had, making many earnest promises, shoving him out, and closing the door upon him. But the bombilation across the way abated not a semiquaver.

I could stand no more. Seizing my hat, and sheltering the iniquitous nickel in a forgiving palm, I went for walk and some bananas. I had long since discovered the wonderful nutritive value of bananas, and that a small quantity was amazingly satisfying I knew full well.

I paced off two miles of lake front, bought the bananas on the return trip, and headed for a public square near the Parthenon to make a meal of them.

Now, in this particular square there were just two benches, one at either end. Entering, I noticed that one was amply occupied by three nonworking-men, the other being vacant.

As I approached the vacant one I descried a girl, well-dressed, apparently good-looking, and also carrying a paper bag, an equal distance the other side of it and walking toward me. We reached our goal simultaneously. She stopped. I stopped. The bench was very short. She sat down. I sat down. The bench was very short.

I stood up foolishly and unnecessarily begged her pardon. And then she looked up, and I saw her eyes. They were truly the most beautiful eyes I had, or have, ever beheld.

Brown, they were, and tender; as tender and brown as—as—being hungry at the moment, I could think of no comparison save a piece of old Aunt Mehitiba's delicious fried chicken, than which nothing was ever a more gloriously golden-brown.

A minute she appraised me; then, evidently satisfied I was not one of those city pests known as male flirts, she turned impersonally away, and with queenly dignity granted me a place beside her. Instantly I thanked her and sat down. A minute passed. I wondered would it offend her should I speak to her again. I considered offering her a banana. I always prefer conviviality to solitude when dining. At length I uncovered my dinner and spread it before her.

"Won't you take one?" I begged, appreciating the while how exquisitely her tawny mass of hair set off the milky whiteness of her skin, "The Greeks particularly recommended them."

She turned slowly round, glanced at the proffered fruit, then at me. Then she smiled.

"Why, yes, thank you," she replied pleasantly, "if you will have one of my cakes." I thought I detected in her voice the soft, lazy drawl of the Southern bred.

She opened the paper bag she had been holding tightly and held it toward me. It contained a half dozen or so tiny coconut-frosted cakes. I took one. Conversation languished—collapsed, in fact. Of course, the next logical subject should have been a comment on the state of the weather; but I would molest no topic so universally abused and outraged. Wherefore I munched my meal in silence until inspiration came.

"Nice cakes," said I.

"Yes," said she, holding out the bag.

"Thank you, I will," said I, suiting action to acceptance. "They go well with bananas," I pursued. "Like ham with eggs, or butter with biscuits, or—take another one, please—a banana, I mean."

"They do affiliate nicely," she agreed, accepting the invitation. "Still," she amended whimsically, "the amalgamation is not quite so satisfying as certain others I might mention."

"'Tis not," I smiled with a valiant charge at jocosity, "so wide as a porterhouse steak, nor yet so deep as a bowl of vegetable soup, but 'twill serve," said I, "in a pinch."

Her hand paused on its way to the cake bag. She looked at me steadily, her eyes winking rapidly; and when I saw her lip tremble also, I had the absurd notion that she was about to cry. Plainly my waggishness had fallen flat.

"Oh!" she gasped, closing the bag quickly and gripping it tightly, "oh, how can you jest about such things!"

I looked at her sharply. A sudden and awful suspicion dawned upon me. I knew several girls who labored for art's sake, and little else, in the Parthenon. I knew what life meant to young girls in a big city.

"Tell me," I demanded imperatively, "have you eaten any dinner today?"

Her face crimsoned. Then daintily tucking a wisp of hair back into place, she turned upon me with a bravely assumed bravado and laughed, I fancied the laugh rang counterfeit. There seemed no mirth behind it.

"Dinner!" she echoed derisively and laughed again. "Why, I've had no lunch yet—no, nor breakfast, either!"

Then, with a sudden blaze of defiance: "Now is your curiosity satisfied? You've made me tell you something I wouldn't have had my dearest friend know. I'm hungry, actually hungry! I suppose it's because you're a stranger," she went on in a musing tone, "and as I never expect to see you again it doesn't matter much. Will you leave me now, please? I would rather be alone. If you attempt to lend me money I shall scream for a policeman. Here, take your bananas and go."

Before she finished speaking I had stood up and placed the last of the bananas in her lap.

"Don't you dare move an inch," I commanded, "until I come back. I won't be fifteen minutes, and when I return you and I'll go have a big meal some place. I'll get references and a chaperone, if you insist upon 'em," I called back as I turned and hurried off,

I dashed into my studio, took in the semi-bare room with distracted look and sinking heart. It was nearly a month since I had heard from home, and almost everything pawnable was gone. My eye fell upon a suit of armor standing majestically in a corner. There was no time for second thoughts. I hastily took it to pieces and, without bothering to wrap it up, staggered down the stairs with it, and around the corner to a neighborly pawnbroker.

"How much?" I demanded of the sleek Hebrew.

"Three dollar."

"Well, hurry it along."

The armor had cost me thirty a month before.

With the three dollars in my pocket, I made a Chicagoese sprint for the square. Half a block away I saw the girl was gone. The bench was empty. Was I keenly disappointed and chagrined? Yes.

Drawing nearer, I perceived something pinned to the back of the bench. It was the paper bag the cakes had come in, and on it was written these words:

> I have gone to dinner with a friend, who came by shortly after you left. Thank you very much just the same for your kindness.

Such good news should have pleased me, you say? Well, it didn't. Quite the contrary. I could think only of my precious armor pawned for this—a few scribbled words on a scrap of paper.

Then to my disgust I found myself wondering if her friend were a man, wondering if she cared for him, wondering—

"Pish!" I exclaimed, and tore up the paper and started for Giacomo's thirty-five-cent table d'hôte, an unpretentious place much frequented by Bohemians of strong digestions and weak pocketbooks.

But when almost there a reckless impulse laid violent hands on me. It was not often I was attacked by reckless impulses, and when one did grab me I generally succumbed without a struggle.

Therefore, I walked straight past Giacomo's without so much as a side glance, and marched on up the avenue to where thrived a big, glittering, gold-and-white cafe in which one might purchase a rather decent meal, with salted almonds and inky coffee, for a couple of dollars or three.

I entered boldly, handed the not necessarily obsequious waiter my hat as though I intended to give him a three-dollar tip later on, sat down, and perused the menu with just the proper suggestion of a slight scowl.

When the servitor came with napkin and iced water I sat back in my chair and glanced around the dining room, and in doing so I looked straight into the soft, dark eyes of the—yes, it was none other. She sat facing me, a few tables away.

Opposite her sat a man in evening clothes, who, judging from a rear view of him, must have been between twenty and sixty and inclined to shortness and rotundity of figure. His clean red neck over-puckered his low white collar in little fat folds, he had no ears to speak of, and I was reminded of a superb and well-scrubbed prize pig.

I bowed to her as pleasantly as I knew how, again admired her eyes, and ordered some fried chicken.

Now, according to all erotic tradition from the time of Adam and Eve to the Gould family, I should

have had dreams that night.

I broke no traditions. I had the dreams.

As I remember them, they formed a sort of weird, medieval melodrama, the principal characters being a beautiful girl with startled brown eyes, whose role was to flee in terror; a monstrous ogre with fat creases on his neck, whose part was to pursue the girl; and myself, clad in a suit of mail and armed with a pawnbroker's ticket and a bag of bananas, whose role was to defy the ogre. Like all dreams, it had a peculiar ending.

The girl turned into a paintbrush, the ogre into an envelope, and I was rubbing my eyes and yawning at the paintbrush, which lay on the floor, and at the envelope, which lay just beyond it where the postman had pushed it under the door.

It was an expected remittance from home. After breakfast I redeemed the armor and divers other articles, worked on my masterpiece till afternoon, then went to the square.

An hour or more I sat there, quite alone, until a fat, blear-eyed person in tattered habiliments, whose breath awoke memories of a slumming trip I once made to Hinky Dink's barroom, settled himself beside me, begged a match, and after a few general remarks, begged a dime.

I gave it to him and left in disgust. He reminded me of last night's ogre.

I felt vaguely dissatisfied as I walked back to my studio, though I hardly know why. Surely I shouldn't have been so nettled because a tramp chose to sit beside me.

Everything seemed to get out of joint that day. Outside the door I found the rent collector, and inside three overdue bills. Later I discovered my best velveteen jacket had been gnawed by rats. I cast it aside and sat down at my easel to snatch the dying moments of light. I had scarcely put brush to canvas when the frenzied pianist broke loose.

Came a familiar knock at the door.

I put aside my palette, heaved a sigh of resignation, and said, "Come in, Bliffins," in a voice Patient Griselda would have thrilled to hear. Bliffins entered.

Bliffins had a very small room on the top floor, and wrote plays and novels and magazine poetry, and lived mostly on cheese and beans, and had his walls papered with the most interesting collection of rejection-slips I have ever encountered.

He sat down in my easiest chair, leaned back contentedly, and reached for my tobacco jar.

"Well, how're they coming, old scout?" he inquired cordially, tamping the tobacco in his battered brier pipe with a blunt thumb.

"You never vary that formula of yours, do you,

Bliffins?" I observed politely. "Of course, it's no wonder your stuff's refused, if you show no more originality in your writing than you do in your greeting."

Bliffins stared at me in pained surprise. In the Parthenon flummery was the rule, and calumny the exception.

"What's the matter, Jeff?" he asked wonderingly. "Isn't the work going well?"

"Work!" I snorted. "Work with that rackety-bang-bang-bang thundering in the index?" I waved my hand toward the window whence issued the uproar. "Don't ask foolish questions, Bliffins."

Bliffins lighted his pipe and walked over to the window.

"Pretty rough," he announced, after listening a moment, "pretty rough. I'm no connoisseur in music, or even a dilettante, but to my untutored ear this noise soundeth rotten." Then abruptly changing the subject: "I haven't dined yet, Jeff. Got any grub round here?"

"Take this bill and buy some stuff while I get things ready," I answered.

Bliffins was always at his best whenever he was eating. I often reflected upon the stir he would have made in the world of letters had nature so equipped him as to enable him to put his thoughts on paper while putting food into his stomach.

All during our meal he kept up a running fire of comments that were brilliant, entertaining, diverting—and mostly about mine art. For he could hold forth on tone, technique, shading, and so on, quite as glibly as I myself could; and the more he talked the more I appreciated the fact that before I was many years older I would have Rembrandt, Vandyke, and that bunch looking like decorators of souvenir postcards.

But it was after dinner, when we had lighted our pipes and tilted back our chairs and propped our feet on the dining table, that Bliffins had his great inspiration.

"Jeff," he exclaimed suddenly, sitting upright and puffing like a ten-horse-power automobile taking a fifty-horse-power grade, "I've got an idea."

"Hold on to its tail!" I advised excitedly. "What is it? A historical novel without a heroine, or a short story with a logical climax?"

"Hush, child! I mind me of the musicale."

At that moment the demoniacal pianist threw off his temporary restraint, and great billows of discord and clangor came bounding across the air-shaft, through the open window, and into the studio.

"Go on," I urged. "I'll stop at nothing short of manslaughter."

Bliffins leaned back comfortably and again propped his feet on the table.

"Buried somewhere in the rubbish of my abode," he resumed, "is a diabolical musical contrivance, part accordion, part something else, I don't know what, which, if I judge aright, has not uttered a squeak since the battle of Bunker Hill. Which is all the better. Ever play an accordion, Jeff?"

"The nearest I ever got to one," I answered, "was the show-window of a Wabash Avenue music store."

"Better still," pronounced Bliffins. "Wait a minute while I fetch it."

I waited twenty minutes while Bliffins fetched it. In those twenty minutes I had ample time to regulate. Louder and louder the clamor grew, until it reached the proportion of a St. Louis cyclone.

Then entered Bliffins, bearing an odd-looking object about four feet by two that would have gladdened the heart of a lover of antiques. A conservative estimator would have judged its age to be two hundred years.

Bliffins placed the curio in my hands.

"See what you can do with it, Jeff." I slipped my hands under the straps at either end, pressed my fingers against some little buttons, and squeezed it. It issued a hoarse yelp that sounded not unlike the cry of a sea lion just before the keeper arrives with the fish.

"Good! Now, then, go to the window and do your worst. I'll bet you could out-whoop the hullabaloo of a Republican caucus with T. R. running for a third term.

To my surprise, I hesitated.

"Isn't this a rather mean trick, Bliff?" Bliffins shrugged his shoulders.

"Suit yourself, Jeff. It's up to you."

Thus encouraged, I hesitated no longer. I stepped to the window, seized a propitious moment, and began pumping that cacophonous bellows for all it was worth—and in a noise-producing way it was

worth a considerable deal. It boomed and pealed like a sort of combined hurdy-gurdy and sick church organ.

I sha'n't attempt to describe the awful duet. Words would be useless, anyway.

I shall only observe that I came off victorious. I was not aware that I had vanquished my foe, so vociferous was I, and was doing arm-gymnastics with a feverish ferocity, when I felt a hand on my shoulder and heard Bliffins shouting above the din:

"For Heavens sake, come off, Jeff! You've won."

So, indeed, I had. The pianist had ceased. I put down the accordion, shook hands with Bliffins, took the water-pitcher, and went for the beer.

We celebrated our victory in fitting wise, Bliffins giving me a detailed history of the accordion after quaffing his third glass.

"And so it was this old humming-box," ended Bliffins, laying his hand affectionately on the instrument, "that kept General Washington and his men from giving way to despondency at Valley Forge. My great-grandmother told my grandmother, who told my mother, who also told me all about it."

"It has served well in a second battle," I remarked.

"Better keep it here," advised Bliffins. "Methinks this was but a skirmish tonight; the war will follow."

"No doubt, no doubt."

I hung the ancient organ over the armor that night, looked triumphantly at the darkened window across the air-shaft, went to bed, and slept soundly—undisturbed by my unmusical neighbor for the first time in many weeks.

Next day I toiled steadily at my masterpiece, not abating my labor until afternoon, when I closed up shop for a walk. I terminated it at the square.

The brown-eyed girl was sitting on the bench.

No, my heart did not go pit-a-pat, nor did my pulse quicken, nor did my face go red—none of those things which you often read about in light summer fiction happened. I remember taking a note of it at the time.

"I was very much disappointed the other afternoon," I began, sitting down beside her, "when I came back and found you gone."

"I'm sorry," she murmured, in about the same sort of tone she would probably use in saying, "How much is this brown ribbon, please?"

"I wanted the pleasure of taking you to dinner myself."

"And you had to eat alone. I'm sorry."

"And I'm sorry that you are sorry," said I. "I enjoyed a very good meal, thank you kindly."

"U-u-u-m."

"Still, it was rather fortunate—for you, I mean—that a friend came along at such an opportune mo-ment. It was better than dining with a stranger, of course. And for that dispensation of providence I am glad."

"And I am glad that you are glad," she smiled, evincing, I thought, a little less austerity. "I was really somewhat appalled," she went on, "at the thought of dining with a young man whom I had never before seen."

Slightly discomfited, I cast about for a fresh topic. My eye fell upon the prismatic signs of a drugstore opposite the square.

"If I mistake not, there is a soda-fountain in that drugstore yonder," said I. "Suppose we go over and have a—have something. Your former vindication of refusal is weightless now, you know. I am no longer a man whom you have never seen before."

A full minute ticked off before she replied, and when she arose and looked down at me I thought I detected a twinkle of mischief in her fine eyes.

"Very well," she said. "Come on."

As we were leaving the drugstore, after imbibing some purplish concoction unknown in my philosophy, I said:

"It is a beautiful spring day"—and it was—"let's go up to Lincoln Park. It is glorious now—all green and fresh in its vernal dress." (I considered that rather neat at the time.) "Will you go?"

She stepped back to glance at the drugstore clock, then joined me, all eagerness.

"Indeed, I will. I have never been to Lincoln Park, and I am very anxious to see it."

"You are a stranger in Chicago, then?" I ventured, as we started north. I had suggested a streetcar, but she preferred walking the ten blocks or so.

"Just three weeks ago today I had my first glimpse of it, so you may account me a stranger in your fair city."

"Don't call it my fair city," I protested. "It's not mine. I hail from St. Elmo, Tennessee."

She stopped and turned to me with a newborn interest.

"Do you know, I had thought that! And I am from Virginia—Westmoreland County."

"I'd known that long ago," I answered complacently, and indeed I had guessed it.

Before we reached the park we had become pretty well acquainted. She was in Chicago to look after some business interests of her father, who had been too ill to attend in person. Her presence in the city thenceforth would possibly be demanded indefinitely.

Like myself, she received periodic remittances from her family—who had owned a homestead along the Potomac for two hundred years or more. On the day I first saw her the fortnightly check had been delayed, lost, stolen, or gone astray, hence the absence of dinner money.

Her name was Muriel—Muriel Rutledge.

Theretofore I had never given much thought to the beauty of Muriel as a Christian name for a girl, but now I began to discern undreamt-of charms and sweetness in it. In fact, I soon became aware that it was quite the most beautiful girl's name in the world.

Considering divers notions, I decided to make no mention of my career. It would be better, I reflected, to wait until we were—until we had become longer acquainted, and I had become famous, and then tell her all about it.

This idea so pleased me that I even went to the length of informing her I was contemplating legal study, and was in Chicago to that end, thinking the while on the far cry from law to art, and what a delightful denouement mine would be.

Happy, we two, in Lincoln Park that afternoon? Well, I should say!

You may well believe we came to know each other rather well, when, while watching the antics of a lubberly bear and my thoughts somehow reverted to the man in the restaurant and the subsequent ogre, I playfully asked her who her "fat friend" was.

I fancied she seemed a bit disconcerted, for I saw her white teeth pressing upon her under lip in embarrassment—or perhaps it was displeasure at my flippant tone.

"He is—he is a friend of my father," she replied slowly, looking away as she spoke. Suddenly she turned back to me, and I was puzzled to see that she was blushing furiously. "Have you the time, Mr. Mayfair?"

I had redeemed it that morning. I told her it was six.

Instantly she was in a little flutter of consternation.

"Gracious! I'd no idea it was so late. Six o'clock! And I've an engagement for five Which way is the car? I must hurry."

The walk to Clark Street wasn't much of a success. I was in no mood for conversational banter, and she was obviously too perturbed to think of amenities.

While we stood waiting for the streetcar, I blurted out:

"It may seem presumptuous and over-inquisitive of me, Miss Rutledge, but just whom are you going to see?"

Again I saw the warm color flood her face, and again she bit her lip as though painfully confused.

"It would hardly enlighten you," she answered, "even though I told you his name. I am sure you do not know him."

"So it is a man, then," I said sternly.

"Yes, it is a man."

"Tell me," I begged, "not the fat man? Please, not that?"

"He is the one," she answered in a low voice.

"Do you mean to tell me," I began angrily, "that you go to see men—"

"Yes!" She threw up her head defiantly, and the challenge in her eyes checked my galloping tongue. "I mean to tell you just that. I should have been there an hour ago, and he will be very angry with me, and you, I think, are partly to blame, and—and here's my car, thank goodness."

Silently, I helped her to the platform. The conductor rang his bell. The car moved on.

I was stung to a panic. She was leaving me—perhaps forever!

"Will you be at the bench tomorrow?" I shouted foolishly.

She either did not hear or did not deign to answer.

She was gone, and I was staring after the rumbling streetcar which bore her away, and wondering if it could be possible that I, plain Jefferson Davis Mayfair, had inadvertently stumbled upon one of those baffling mysteries, or upon one of those shocking tragedies, one daily sees scare-headed in the saffron journals, and had as inadvertently stumbled out of it again.

CHAPTER II

Ear-piercing war raged that night.

My tuneless foe, of course, opened first fire. I rushed to the firing line my heavy artillery, and sent back as bad as I received, or worse.

It was an unearthly hullabaloo. To the harsh clash of chords a back-fence tabby added its mournful caterwauling; then a forsaken dog chimed in with a melancholy yowl; windows were thrown up, and

gruff-voiced epithets struck a crescendo note in the diabolical discord.

Bliffins, wearied of knocking unheeded, opened the door and came in.

"Go to it, Jeff, go to it!" he encouraged enthusiastically. "You'll win out yet, old scout."

"If I don't, I'll die fighting," I shouted over my shoulder. "I'm going to conquer this thing, I tell you, if I have to hire a brass band."

As though cowed by this formidable war-cry, my adversary immediately ceased firing.

I put the accordion away and rinsed out the water-pitcher. Once again Bliffins and I quaffed the beer of victory.

Of course I went to the square next afternoon. I always did. Both benches were vacant, but I soon saw to it that one of them was fully occupied. This so that passersby would keep on passing.

The first half hour tripped pleasantly by. Anticipation is a wonderful thing. The second half-hour not quite so trippingly. And the fourth half-hour was a sluggard and snail, and its creepy shuffle and crawl the quintessence of misery and chagrin.

Then I began to get angry with myself. I had met pretty girls before—girls almost, if not quite, as pretty as she. None of them had turned my head. I had always escaped unscathed.

Wherefore, then, should I allow this? No! It should not be. I jumped up, started home, fiercely torturing the question.

Somehow it would not work. I was dull and lugubrious when I reached my studio. I scarcely noticed a most imperative dun for money that lay on the threshold; and when later Bliffins found me sitting gloomily in the dark, with the clamorous enemy in full cry and possession of the field, he was no more surprised than I. I had not known it.

Next afternoon, suddenly rounding a corner near the square, I came plump upon her.

She was dressed (as I discovered later) in an exquisite gown of some soft, shimmering brown stuff, and wore a marvelously becoming hat.

Yes—it was true, what the summer authors said— about the pit-a-pat heart and the quickening pulse, and all the rest.

I experienced all the emotions simultaneously, and I felt like shaking hands with all the summer authors. They understood. They knew.

As we walked to a bench and sat down, she kept chattering away volubly upon random topics, but underneath it all I plainly detected a nervousness, an uneasiness—even a fear.

It was easily to be seen she was endeavoring to mask with an outward volatility some inward perturbation. Again my mind's eye saw the yellow journal horror-heads, and a great wave of love and pity surged over me. I longed to protect her, to implore her to tell me all—no matter what that all might be.

To my disgust I did nothing of the sort. When I spoke it was merely to ask her if she would go with me to a certain amusement park which had opened a few days before.

"I've never been," I explained, "but I understand it's hilarious fun, though rather bourgeois, no doubt. Will you come?"

"Of course I will. I've never been, either, but I've often heard of it, and I am sure it must be enchanting."

It was. We took in everything, from the four-legged duck to the Perilous Plunges for Plucky People, and the next morning I pawned a pearl scarf-pin.

After three or four ecstatic hours that were so many minutes, came the same black cloud that had darkened day before yesterday's sky of serenity. We were; watching the lady divers when she turned to me and asked:

"What time is it, Mr. Mayfair?"

"Why bother about time?" said I. "There's plenty of it left. Here, take another piece of this yum-yum candy and watch Mlle. Aquazelle. She's going to do a triple somersault now."

"No, really, Mr. Mayfair, I must know."

"Very well then," I sighed, and consulted my watch. "It's five-thirty-seven."

"Heavens! And it's five miles to the Loop. Oh, I must fly!"

"Now, look here," I demanded, "don't you go and tell me you have another appointment with—"

"The fat man?" she smiled. "Yes, I have. And I must hurry, too. Let us take the Elevated. It's the quickest."

We took it without a word. But as we went skimming toward town I uttered the question that had been a maggot in my brain for the last two days and nights.

"Muriel," I entreated, and her first name slipped out unconsciously, so often had I called her so to myself, "Muriel, won't you please tell me just who this person is?"

"Why certainly," she answered quickly, then stopped and looked down. A wave of color dyed her face crimson. Her embarrassment was pitiful.

"Don't tell me unless you want to," I said gently.

"Why, surely there is no reason why I shouldn't." She looked up inquiringly. "He i-is—" She faltered and stopped; then turned and looked out of the window. "He is father's attorney. There!" She turned back to me, smiling and dimpling. "Now the mystery is all cleared away."

Her counterfeit levity gradually died at my expression. I wanted to say: "Why will you lie to me, girl? Why not tell me the truth?" for I knew in my heart that she was uttering a falsehood.

But I assumed a playful tone, which I knew rang false as a leaden dollar, and asked:

"Will it ever be possible, do you think, to see you some time or other when you have no immediate engagement with this—attorney?"

She knitted her brow thoughtfully. Heavens, I thought she must be with him always. And she can't be engaged to him. She would tell me if she were.

Then I became aware that she was speaking.

"Let me see," she began contemplatively, "this is Friday, the twenty-eighth; tomorrow I have—have business to attend to; Sunday is letter-writing day; Monday, more business; Tuesday—u-u-m! Yes, Tuesday, there is nothing on—Tuesday, June first."

"You are quite positive?" I insisted listlessly.

"Quite."

"All's well, then." I strove to speak joyfully, but I know my voice held no enthusiasm. "The first of June shall be our day."

"All to ourselves," said she.

"All to ourselves," I repeated.

With that we parted.

More and more I felt myself being drawn into the meshes of some inexplicable, perhaps tragical, mystery. Once I paused, fired with an impulse to play the spy upon her. But I quietly put it aside as cowardly and unworthy, and caught the surface-car for home.

For the first time since getting my first box of water-color paints I could rouse no interest in art.

CHAPTER III

A memorable day was June the first. Chronologically, I must write down the events

First, I sold a painting. (Put that in *italics*, Mr. Printer, please.) *I sold a painting.*

It was a still-life painting, one I had worked on for a month and a half, and I got twelve dollars ready money for it. I could hardly contain my joy and jubilation when I opened the thin envelope and found a note from my dealer and a check to my order.

I pranced around my studio like a man gone mad, laughed in my mirror, and exulted in my gift. My friends were right, then. I could paint, after all. Half of the twelve dollars sent telegrams and letters to many St. Elmoans, apprising them of the fact that their quondam townsman was going lickety-split along fame's highway.

Secondly, I gave the last finishing touch to my masterpiece, which was to be hung in an Amateurs' Exhibit—how I loathed that word amateur!—in the Art Institute.

Last, and far most important of all, the first of June was our day—Muriel's and mine. With the remainder of the twelve dollars, plus a goodly share of money on hand, I hired an automobile, and we went a pleasuring far out along the "North Shore." A glorious day it was, and a glorious trip.

Though it came hard at first, I still forbore to reveal my great secret. Once I thought of doing so, but the fine edge of enravishment had now worn off, and I could view the matter with a cooler eye. No, it were better to not tell her yet. I would wait until I had achieved something truly great.

On the way back we stopped at a roadhouse for dinner, and there I did a mad thing. It may have been the reaction of the morning's elation, it may have been the witchery of the wine, it may have been the exquisite loveliness of her in the soft candlelight— whatever the incitement, I asked her to marry me.

No sooner were the words uttered than I could have bitten my tongue out for giving them birth. I didn't want to marry. Men with careers shouldn't marry. Men who couldn't support wives and families shouldn't marry.

Of course she would say "yes." I never doubted that. What man ever does?

Then through the turmoil of my thoughts drifted the consciousness that she was speaking; and—hallo! what's this—she was refusing me; actually refusing me! Me, who was destined to be America's foremost artist! Odzookens!

She looked down as she spoke, fingering a thin-stemmed glass beside her plate.

She liked me very much—more, indeed, than any boy she could think of just then, and she had always intended, if ever she married, that it should be a Southern man, but she did not want to marry—yet.

She was too young—we were both too young—to think of such a thing, and wasn't it rather close here, and hadn't we better be going?

It was. We had. We went.

Heavy silence marked the first half-mile or so. Then poisonous thoughts began to goad my brain. The green-eyed monster dragged his slimy length between us, gnashing his venomous fangs. When I spoke my voice sounded unnatural in my own ears.

"Will you, or will you not, tell me," said I, "who this man is whom you see most every day?"

She did not answer; and the monster of the green eyes flicked his virulent tongue and wrapped me in his noxious embrace.

"What is he to you, this lubberly fellow?"

She turned upon me sharply, and by the light of a passing auto I saw her eyes flashing angrily.

"That will do," she said icily. "I have told you once that he is—"

"He is not!" I exclaimed. "He is no more your father's attorney than I am. Of that I am sure. You are concealing something from me. But why? Won't you please tell me why, Muriel?"

"I will not. Furthermore, I wish you to drop the subject."

"Then I am to infer," I began hotly, "that you and this man—"

"You are to infer nothing," she blazed furiously. "Don't you ever speak to me again. I hate you! I never want to see you again—never! Stop and let me out."

"I shall do nothing of the sort. I'm going to take you home. Rest assured I sha'n't break your mandate."

Nor did I. She alighted at some point on the North Side—I scarce knew where, nor cared—and we parted without so much as a frigid farewell.

I told the chauffeur to turn back and drive through the park until I commanded him to stop.

Rolling softly over the macadamized driveway, I marked out my course. I would renounce all worldly pleasures, abjure all creature comforts; body and soul I would give myself to my art.

I would become celebrated. And, when I had become famous I would go to her and say, "Ha! madam. I once asked you to marry me, did I not?" Then I would bow stiffly and leave her to her unhappiness.

With this grim determination I went to bed that night. The room opposite was dark; there was no piano performance; I slept soundly. Next day's early morning inaugurated my rigorous resolve.

Eighteen hours a day, seven days a week, I toiled. With the exception of Bliffins and the postman, I barred my door to all callers. I went no more to the square. I gave up walking, attic-talking, my onetime haunts, my rambling jaunts.

Work, work, work, was my fetish. And worship it I did, from blush of dawn till eventide, and from eventide till mid of night. I slung more paint in a single day than the average artist slings in a week.

But alas and alas! Though my friends continued to admire, though my family continued to uphold, though Bliffins continued to enthuse, I began to have the terrifying feeling that I was dashing full tilt against inevitable, inexorable defeat. My paintings simply would not sell.

The dealer who tried to sell them began to return them, brutally informing me they cluttered up his place and were a drug on the market. When I learned from this same dealer that the one picture I had sold—one of an overturned basket of fruit— had been bought by a rich pork-packer to hang over a grease-spot in his kitchen, I was no longer inspirited by memories of that eventful first of June.

One day at duskfall, as I was hurrying home with a loaf of bread, I stopped a moment at the square. From behind a hedge I saw Muriel.

It may have been my imagination, but fancied she looked careworn and unhappy, and she seemed so friendless and woebegone, sitting there alone with the shadows gathering thick about her. I wondered if she had missed me. I felt myself slipping, slipping, slipping— But resolutely I broke away and hurried back to a beef stew I had left simmering on the stove.

Climbing the stairs, I overtook the postman, who handed me a letter. A glance showed me it was from bachelor Uncle Bob, who owned a chicken-farm in Kentucky, had the gout, a few butter-tubs full of money, and a heart as mellow as his ripest bourbon. By the light of the kerosene lamp I read his letter:

Dear Jefferson :

Your mother and sisters write me that you are not doing over well in Chicago—financially, I mean.

Now I know little or nothing about pictorial art and kindred matters, and it is not for me to counsel young talent, but I have a proposition, which, if you be in need of ready money, may strike you not unfavorably.

My doctor has ordered me to Carlsbad, and his decree must be obeyed. I'll have to leave somebody in charge here. What do you say?

I'll pay you $75 a month and all expenses, and if you show any chicken-raising ability, I'll turn the whole thing over to you. I'll have to give it to somebody sometime, of course, and I know of no one I would rather see have it than you.

Let me hear from you, boy, as soon as possible.
    Affectionately,

Uncle Bob.

P. S.—Six hundred fowls the first six months would be doing very fair for a beginner.

Three months before I would have been affronted by this. Not so now. Now I found myself speculating upon things.

Statistics occurred to me: If you broke the eggs laid in one year by the great American hen you'd have an omelet big enough to cover the State of Texas, or if all the roosters in the United States perched on the Masonic Temple tomorrow morning and rendered a cooperative crow, the cock-a-doodle-do would make the roar of the elevated railroad in Wabash Avenue sound like the chirp of a sparrow in Van Buren Street. And so on.

I sniffed the aroma from the stew-pot. Now, it wouldn't be disagreeable if there was a plump pullet in that pot instead of potatoes and onions and twelve-cent beef.

But the aspiration of years is not to be overthrown in a minute's time. It was with a sick heart that I sat down after dinner and replied to Uncle Bob's letter. I told him merely that I would think the matter over and let him know.

After sealing and stamping the envelope, I lighted my pipe, leaned back, and let my gaze wander round the studio. Appalling heaps of pictures—the tremendous achievement of Herculean labor—were stacked around the walls. Bliffins had praised them all. My friends had assured me they were sure to be good. My family, too. But the public and my dealer thought not so.

I sat up suddenly. Was their criticism honest? Was it sincere? Was it not biased? Possibly—very possibly.

One set opined I was an embryonic Michelangelo, the other believed I was a misguided dauber of backyard fences. Both, I was inclined to believe, were wrong, one because it knew me, the other because it knew me not.

What I needed was an unprejudiced, impartial, and efficient judge. One who would not declare me a tyro because my name was unknown, nor yet adjudge me an unappreciated genius because none would buy my art.

Ensued a museful space.

Muriel? Why not? She had an eye for beauty. She would know a good painting from a bad. She knew not what I was. Yes, Muriel should be the judge. Her viewpoint would be neutral, her verdict just. If for me—art! If against me—chickens!

So I tore up my letter to Uncle Bob.

Next afternoon I was waiting in the square when Muriel arrived. She stopped at sight of me, took a fal-

tering step, then turned and hastened quickly away.

In three seconds I was beside her, bridging our hiatus with no waste material.

"Will you go with me to the Art Institute?" I asked breathlessly.

No answer. She continued to walk on swiftly. I kept step with her, using persuasion as best I might.

"There are such a number of good oils on view," I pleaded, "and I know your love for the artistic. I thought perhaps—"

She stopped and looked at me very calmly.

"Didn't I command you to never speak to me again?" she asked in a very chilly voice.

"You did," said I.

"And you promised you never would," she observed, then turned abruptly and reentered the square.

"I know I did, Muriel," I acknowledged humbly, quickly overtaking her, "but I simply can't stand it any longer. I've tried and I can't. You don't want to be responsible for breaking a fellow's heart, do you? Well, that's what you're doing to me—breaking my heart."

Why detail? I knew I had won after that. An hour later we were strolling chattily down a corridor of the Art Institute, where, in the amateur show, some of my pictures hung. Gradually, diplomatically, I led her to the room where hung my masterpiece, companioned by certain of my lesser paintings.

"Now, there's something," said I, nodding toward a horrific conception of the Spanish Inquisition, "that seems tolerably well done."

She turned and appraised it. I felt myself trembling with a fever of apprehension. A minute passed. It seemed a year. Lord! Would the girl never speak?

She didn't. She laughed. My heart turned to lead.

"W-why do you laugh?" I faltered.

"Because it's so funny," she answered simply,

swallowing hard.

"Funny!" I gasped. "Why, yes. It is so obviously amateurish it is really ludicrous. I know it's mean to laugh, but sometimes one cannot control one's risibility. I wonder who is responsible for such a daub?"

She stepped nearer to learn the artist's name.

"And this one over here?" I interposed hastily, leading her away. "What think you of that?"

Another silent appraisal. Another palpitation. Then she turned to me, and once again I saw mirth in her eyes. As in a dream I heard her say:

"It is even worse than the other." And she laughed.

I could bear little more. Yet took I her arm fiercely, and with a sick heart led her to my masterpiece. Upon this all now depended. I pointed to it silently and looked a question at her.

A long while she regarded the painting. Then she spoke.

"What a great pity," she said in a low voice.

The blue devils went scampering from me, and a great gladness sang in my soul, for it was a most piteous and pathetic fancy I had depicted on my canvas.

"What a pity," she went on, "to expend so much labor, so much paint, and good canvas for such a hopeless, irremediable failure. It is sad. Let us move on; let us look at something worth while. I've seen enough of this shallow display."

"No," said I, shaking my head wearily, "let us go home. For the shock of doom has sounded, and I am very tired—very dreadfully tired."

CHAPTER IV

On some pretext or other, I sent Muriel home in a cab, went to a telegraph office, and wired Uncle Bob thus:

Accept. Leave for Bowling Green tomorrow night.

Then I went to my studio. I was standing, the incarnation of despondency, before a half-finished painting on my easel when Bliffins knocked.

I paid no heed. He again knocked, then opened the door and entered. He came over to me and stood looking over my shoulder a moment.

"It's a daisy, Jeff," he said confidently, patting me on the back in his usually unctuous manner, "a daisy."

I turned upon him sharply.

"It is, eh? Well, here's where the daisy withers."

Fiercely I seized from the table a carving-knife, and eight, nine, ten times plunged it through the canvas. Then, while the mood was yet strong upon me, I kicked the easel across the room, lugged from a corner a huge pile of dust-covered paintings, and one by one ripped them to pieces with the cleaver, piling the debris in the middle of the floor.

Mouth agape, eyes distended, Bliffins stood staring at me in dumb amazement.

"Don't stand there like a cigar Indian," ordered I. "Get busy."

"H-how, Jeff?"

"You might pile this junk in the grate, for one thing, and set fire to it."

"W-what does it all mean, Jeff?"

"It means," I cried bitterly, halting operations to confront him, "that you have lied to me; that others have lied to me, aye, my family—and others.

"I'm no painter. Never was intended to be one. Never could be one. I've wasted two years finding it out. I'm going to raise chickens. And fresh eggs. Art! Bohemia! Temperament! Bosh! Mention those words to me again and I'll do murder."

There came a terrific crash of chords. It was the war-whoop of the thundering pianist. Louder and louder swelled his awful roaring. The battle was on.

I dropped the carving-knife for the accordion and fought furiously.

Bliffins joined me.

Twenty minutes or longer the conflict raged. Then the lights went out of the enemy's camp.

The battle was over.

Heated though I was, I yet was not pleased when Bliffins shouted something not exactly complimentary across the air-shaft.

"Don't taunt a man when you've got him down, Bliffins," said I reprovingly. "That's a coward's act. Come, let's finish wrecking this joint, then we'll have a cake and a bottle of Chianti. It'll be our last together, Bliffy, old boy."

I bought an armful of poultry journals next morning and repaired to the square. About eleven o'clock Muriel sat down beside me on the bench. I saw at a glance that she had been crying.

"Tell me all," I entreated, boldly taking her hand. "I can sympathize. I, too, have had trouble."

Her only answer was to free her hand from mine and turn away. Instantly all those direful, fearful misgivings of some days agone returned to me a dozen fold.

"Is it that odious—" I began heatedly, then stopped.

She had anticipated my next word and was nodding her head violently.

"The beast!" I cried hotly. "What has he done to you? The beast!"

She clenched her little white fists angrily.

"He has been making—he has been trying to make love to me; and I've always detested him—the fat little toad! And he knows it—or should!"

I moved nearer and again took her hand in mine,

"Muriel," I begged, "aren't you ever going to tell me just who and what this person is?"

"He—he— Oh, I've fibbed to you so much I hardly know where or how to begin. He is not an attorney; he does not know my father; he does not know any of my family."

"I had guessed as much. Please go on."

"I'll start at the beginning. I didn't come to Chicago on business; I came for a career. And then I met you, and—and, I hardly know why I did, it; it was silly, I know. I didn't want to tell you of my career; I wanted to wait until I was celebrated, and then dazzle you with my renown. It was silly, don't you think so? And vain, too."

"And this career?" I asked, blushing and waiving her question.

"Music. My family, my friends, told me I was destined to be a great pianist. I became imbued with their rosy enthusiasm. I came to Chicago to study."

"And the fat man?"

"Is—was my music teacher. I rented a piano from him. I installed it in my studio in the Parthenon. Every spare moment I practiced. He continually praised my playing, declared I was born to be one of the truly great; and—poor, deluded me!—I believed him.

"Then came some dreadful person who rented a studio just opposite mine. Nothing but a narrow airshaft separated us. He played—or tried to play—some sort of horrible concertina, or something or other.

"At first I thought he was crazy. But now I know he was not. He was mocking me! He played only when I did. And last night"—there came a catch in her voice which she quickly changed into a cough—"last night he—he shouted at me to shut up!"

She stopped and turned away, and I vowed quick and pitiless vengeance on Bliffins.

"But he was right," she went on spiritedly, turning back to me. "I know now he was right. It was all a mistake. I can't play.

"Everybody has deceived me—everybody except this man. He knew. And now I know, and I have sent my piano back to the warerooms and I never want to see another one again as long as I live, and I want to get away from it all—away from the city and all.

"I'm homesick, Jefferson, very, very homesick."

Yes, as I said in the beginning, there are many sorts of critics, and the best of them all is the intuitive critic.

The first six months we raised seven hundred and fifty chickens.

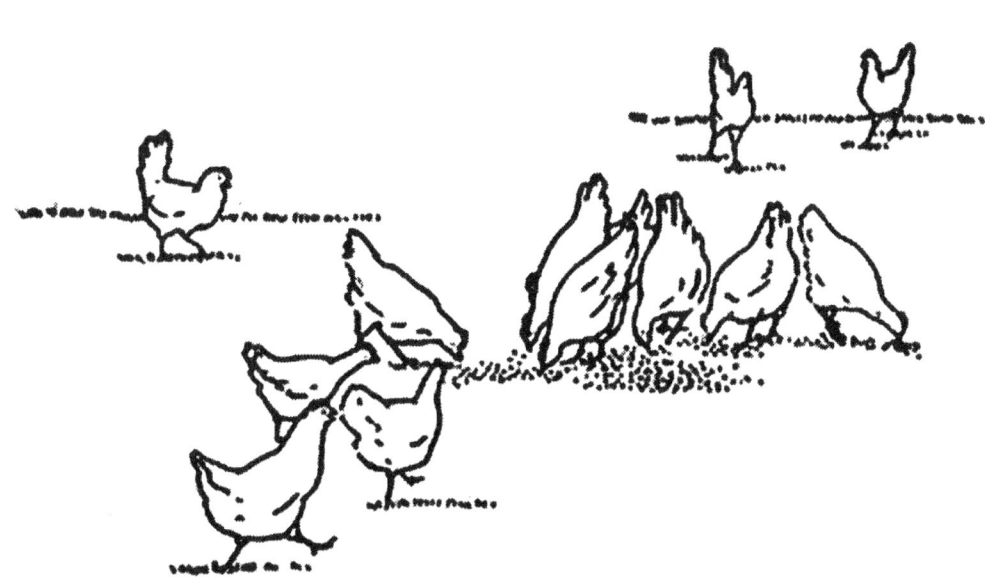

THE MAD DETECTIVE

by John D. Swain

CHAPTER I
THE VACATION

At the top of a little hill, Jed Hooper shut off the engine and brought his crazy flivver to a full stop. He turned in his seat and spoke to the two passengers, buried under a heap of luggage and parcels.

"Yonder's the camp," he said. "The white one, against the clump of cedars."

Frank Weston and his wife gazed with tired eyes over a country well worth coming hundreds of miles to behold. Though fairly well settled, as the Maine countryside goes, it seems almost a primeval wilderness, with most of the farmhouses hidden by the green forest, and only here and there in a clearing, a glimpse of distant homes, with an occasional white spire piercing the treetops. A mile away Frenchman's Bay glowed blue and gold in the afternoon sun, and in the offing Mt. Desert loomed like a huge purple jewel floating lightly on the breast of the Atlantic.

"Why, there's smoke coming from our chimney!"

Jed Hooper looked through his windshield. "Yes, ma'am. My wife reckoned it'd seem homelike to you. She'll have a pot of tea waiting for you, and mebbe some of her molasses cookies. Thoughtful about such things, Lizzie is."

He slipped in the clutch, and the car started, coasting easily down the slope, crossing a noisy little brook, swinging in from the highway over a grass-grown road which brought them through a ragged orchard to the front door of a well-preserved, story-and-a-half frame house badly in need of paint. Half of an old grindstone formed the doorstep, and as the passengers dismounted stiffly, the door opened and a fat, smiling woman wearing a gingham apron beamed on them, and began to help them unload their bundles before the slower-moving Jed had heaved himself out of the car.

"Land sakes! That a cat you got there in that satchel with a little window in it?"

Annie Weston laughed. "Yes, Mrs. Hooper. We thought it wouldn't be homelike without a cat; so we bought one from the animal shop in New York."

Lizzie Hooper lifted the satchel and peered curiously at the alarmed creature which was faintly meowing within.

"Well," she decided. "It ain't much to look at! Got no tail, for one thing. Never could abide a tailless cat.

They look sort of unfinished. If it was your own, one you'd got attached to, I could understand; but why on earth you should go buy one! Up here, we're glad to give 'em away. Why, Jed has got to drown four kittens, right now. Pretty little things they be, too."

"Oh, how dreadful!" Annie Weston cried. "I never could bear to do it!"

"Well, if you had about twelve a year, you'd have to, or the country'd be overrun with wild critters. We got four, right now; and whenever the count runs higher 'n that, there's a drowning has to be tended to."

The city couple entered through the wide doorway, and from its little entry passed into a pleasant, low-ceilinged room in whose far end burned a cheery, open fire. The furniture was simple but effective; little, old, low rockers, with gay chintz covers; a mellow cherry table; a horsehair sofa; a great hooked rug on the floor of wide boards, some samplers and dingy steel engravings on the walls. The table was set out with dishes, cups and saucers; and soon the Westons were devouring fresh molasses cookies, dishes of wild strawberries with cream, cups of strong tea, slices of home-baked bread thickly spread with fresh butter.

After eating, the question of the cat came up. The door was shut, and the animal released, its attention called to a saucer of rich milk. It ignored it and all the inmates with equal impatience and began to circle the room, the fur along its spine raised, whiskers twitching, eager only to find a way out of the room and house.

"That's the way with cats in a strange place," Jed remarked. "They won't settle down till they've learned every nook and hole in the place. You got to butter their paws!"

"You—*what*?" Mrs. Weston gasped. "Butter their—"

"Yes'm. Never fails; you look and see."

With some difficulty Jed succeeded in capturing the frightened, bobtailed gray creature, which he held despite its scratching and wriggling, while Lizzie, with the skill of long practice, took a spoonful of butter from the dish on the table, and thoroughly rubbed it into each one of the four paws. This done, Jed set the cat down.

Instead of running about as before, the cat looked slightly puzzled. It shook first one, then the other of its paws; seated itself, and carefully licked each one clean. The process took some time; and when done, the cat seemed for the first time to notice its saucer of milk. It sniffed daintily at it, found it good, and lapped up the very last drop, as well as another saucerful which Lizzie poured. Thereafter the city cat sat peacefully down beside the fireplace, blinked its eyes, washed its whiskers clean, and began to purr.

"Well, I'll be darned!" said Weston. "How come?"

Jed chuckled. "Seems like the one thing a cat regards above all else, is to clean itself of anything that gits onto it; 'specially its feet. While it was licking off the butter, it forgot it was in a strange place; and the taste of butter made it remember it was hungry. So, having eaten in a place, why, that makes it seem like home. Same as I hope you folks do after eating ma's molasses cakes and tea!"

Annie Weston laughed. "We certainly do, don't we, Frank? You see, this is really our honeymoon! Yes, when we were married all that Frank could spare was just three days. Of course, we went to Atlantic City! And every year since then, we've promised ourselves a real honeymoon. And this is it; we're going to stay two months, and forget business and everything. Going to wear old clothes, and go to bed with the chickens, and rise with the sun. Why, we haven't even subscribed for a daily paper! We've put New York behind us, stock-market reports, theatrical reviews, divorces, crimes and all. It's quiet we want, and just to be ourselves and get acquainted."

Jed and Lizzie both nodded appreciatively.

"Well, you'll git all the quiet you want! Nothing ever happens here more exciting than a hen stealing her nest, or a school of mackerel reported out in the bay, or the like of that. We ain't even had a funeral for more'n a year. Folks live long, up in these parts, even if they don't live very fast!"

While Jed showed Weston about the yard, and explained how to start the wooden pump if it got obstinate, and pointed out the ruinous chicken run and the bearing trees of what had once been a fine fruit orchard, his wife took Mrs. Weston all about the house, with which she fell in love at once. It was primitive to a degree the city woman had never dreamed of; no running water in the house, a wooden sink, scrubbed clean, great beds with queer contraptions of tauted ropes for springs, shelves of quaint old china and pewter, everything immaculately clean, and nothing lacking save modern plumbing and lighting. The latter consisted of old kerosene lamps, and tallow candles.

"It's plain," Lizzie admitted. "But it served old Miss Jarvis more'n fifty years. She was born and died right in this house, and her father before her. This chinaware and the furniture was hers. It all belongs to a niece, who lives out to Minnesota. We have the leasing of the house. An artist had it last summer. He spattered paint some; I cleaned it off as well as I could."

The Hoopers rattled off in their car, cordially urging their tenants to call on them for any help needed. They could supply milk, butter, eggs, vegetables, salt pork, fresh-killed fowls, advice, and back numbers of a weekly newspaper, the Farmer's Almanac, and the Rural Agriculturist.

Alone, for almost the first time in five years, the Westons looked at one another, laughed happily, took hands and executed an improvised dance about their living room, kitchen, and parlor. The cat, already entirely at home, was out in the yard clumsily attempting to catch grasshoppers, an exciting game which had not, in its brief life passed in a bird-and-animal shop, been called to its attention.

"Are you going to be contented, Frank?" his wife asked a little wistfully.

"*Am* I? Why, I've left everything in such shape that I don't even want to see a newspaper; and only half a dozen people have my mail address. That's our mail box, by the way; that galvanized tin out on the gate post, with the little red tin flag sticking up in it. I'm going to loaf and grow fat, and make love to you!"

"You may grow thin, on my cooking! It is years since I touched a frying pan; and then I had an electric range, a cookbook, and all sorts of devices to save labor. You're going to suffer indigestion for a few days, old boy!"

"Well, I'll work it off splitting kindling, and digging clams, and tramping through the woods!"

That evening they ate their first meal alone, with no servant to stand at their elbows, no cook to cater to their whims. And for the first time in long years, both were ravenously hungry. There was a cement-floored, stone-walled little cellar, with only narrow slits for ventilation, and a single door leading from the kitchen; a solid plank of oak, fastened by a hand-wrought iron staple. In the cellar were bins of clean white sand, containing vegetables. There was a keg of cider, and a swing shelf loaded with bottles and jars of jellies, pickles, preserves, relishes, fruits. A big ham swung from an iron hook; underneath stood a keg of salt pork, and a pail of salt mackerel. In the kitchen was flour, sugar, a bread and cake tin, a wood stove and a small oil one. Jed Hooper had caught and cleaned a mess of flounders for them, boiled two fat lobsters, and set a pail of clams by the sink.

Red, with a new burn on one white arm, but radiantly happy withal, Annie flitted back and forth from kitchen stove to table. They had decided to eat in the kitchen; it was large, extending the entire width of the house, and it had a fireplace, as had nearly every room in the house. They ate until they were more than satisfied, but no indigestion resulted, even though the fried potatoes were scorched, and the coffee was too strong.

With the setting of the sun, a chill descended; and they were glad to close the door and sit near the fireplace in the living room.

Romeo the cat, groggy from the amount of grasshoppers he had devoured, dozed at their feet. The wood crackled pleasantly; outside all was still save for the distant hooting of an owl, and once or twice a dry, sharp bark which they supposed to be uttered by a dog, but which was really a young fox out hunting in the moonlight. Then, suddenly and startling, a whip-poor-will began its weird song very near them; stealing to the window, they could just make out its body perched on the old wooden pump.

The cat, whose experience had been only with birds in cages, pricked up his ears and licked his chops. The song of the night warbler drowned the steady ticking of the wooden clock with its picture of a square-rigger on a very wooden sea.

"Sounds sort of lonesome, don't you think?" whispered Annie.

Frank Weston laughed happily.

"Sounds good! Haven't heard one since I was a ten-year-old. Don't believe I've ever thought of one for twenty years. They used to say it is a good sign when one of them comes so near a house. They mostly cling to the deep woods. Guess this one is serenading us, welcoming us home!"

Tired from their long journey, and the excitement of arrival, they went early to bed. Upstairs, in a half-finished attic, were three small chambers, each with its big bed and old-fashioned bureau and washstand with bowl and pitcher. Fine linen towels, hemstitched by Jed Hooper's wife, hung on the racks; new cakes of cheap soap were in their china dishes. Annie chose the rear room, which looked out over distant Frenchman's Bay, now shimmering in moonlight, and separated from them by a heavy growth of cedars. Her husband took the front one which connected with it, the door having been removed from its hinges. The lamps were blown out. Romeo settled himself at the foot of Frank's bed, and began a faint bedtime song. The whip-poor-

will had ceased its welcome; it was intensely still now, outside. Listening closely, Annie could hear from the sea the deep respiration of the making tide as it flung itself against the rocky shore. Her thoughts drifted out on the tides of sleep.

Suddenly, appallingly loud in the quiet night, there came to her ears the heavy drumming of hard knuckles on wood. Downstairs, the front door vibrated to the sound of a knocking that would not be denied!

CHAPTER II
THE WARNING

There was something ominous in that urgent summons, heard in the night. Already the moon was sinking behind the cedar swamp; looking from his window, Frank Weston could make out only masses of shadow relieved by a pallid glimmer that revealed no details. Directly below him, and standing on the old grindstone by the front door, was a dark figure that looked too large to be a man. Who could have any business with them at such an hour, long after the countryside had retired to slumber, the oil lamps blown out in distant windows?

His voice, despite his efforts to control it, quavered a little as he leaned out into the cool night air, and called softly: "Yes? Who is it, and what do you want?"

The man below raised his head to the sound, his face showing as a whitish blur masked in a heavy beard and shaded by an old, floppy, black felt hat.

"Your name Weston? Just got here from the city, ain't ye? Well, I'm Jason Hodge—your nearest neighbor down the road a piece. Come down so's I can talk without hollerin'. Got something important to say, and there's no telling who may be listenin'."

"What is it, Frank? Is anything wrong?"

The anxious voice of his wife came from the adjoining room as Weston hastily slipped into trousers and shoes, not bothering to put on his stockings nor fasten the laces.

"Oh, nothing much, I guess," he answered lightly, though his nerves still jumped a little after being roused so startlingly from profound sleep. "Only a neighbor; says his name is

Hodge. Probably wants to borrow something; folks out in the remote country are always running out of matches or flour or something. It's all right; tell you all about it soon as he's got what he wants and gone home."

He took a pocket torch from the bureau, and snapped on its cold, white beam as he stole down the narrow stairway with its carved mahogany railing, which some misguided tenant had long ago painted white. For just an instant he hesitated at the door, before slipping the heavy iron bolt; then with a smile at his timidity, which he realized came solely from the unfamiliar isolation of one accustomed to living packed in among teeming thousands, he threw open the door. It creaked loudly in the silence; and unconsciously he stepped back a pace, his hand tightening on the metal cylinder of the torch.

The strange caller blinked as the beam played about his rugged, homely face. "I won't step in," he said, his voice pitched cautiously low. "And sorry to wake ye up this time o' night. But fact is, there's trouble afoot. I knew you and your wife just got in today; we see ye pass with Jed Hooper. Wanted to warn ye to keep doors and windows locked tight, and it might not be a bad idee to have a gun handy. Have you got one?"

"I have an automatic," Weston admitted a little sheepishly. "Thought I might amuse myself shooting at a mark. Had it a long time, and never got a chance to fire it off in the city."

The bearded figure nodded. "Mebbe you'll have a real mark to shoot at. Hope not, and tain't likely. This neighborhood is very peaceable. Everybody knows everybody else, or at least, we cal'lated we did. But I just got a telephone message; we've all of us got telephones, but you. That's why I came over to warn ye. Didn't seem right, somehow, with you two city folks sleeping like as not with the door unlocked—which nobody down here ever bothers to lock up nights—"

Weston shivered a little. The chill night air was penetrating his thin shirt and ruffling his thin hair. "But what is it all about? What did you come to warn us about, if the village is as peaceable as you say?"

The bewhiskered man coughed. "That's what I was coming to, mister. As I was saying, I got this telephone message from the sheriff over to Allsworth. That's the county seat. Something terrible has happened at the Bronsons', ten miles away on the Cranberry Beach road. A man—don't know who, because he wore a mask—near killed Mrs. Bronson. This was along about sundown; she only managed to get word through to Allworth half an hour ago. Her husband, Elmer Bronson, was down at the beach, a mile away, floating off that big sloop of his. High tide tonight,

and he's been putting in some new strakes and painting her up. So the Bronson woman was all alone. Well, this stranger, he knocked on her door and asked for a drink of water. Soon as she opened the door and see he was masked, she tried to shut it in his face, but he was too quick for her. Set his foot in the opening and pushed on through. Then seems as if he struck her with something heavy; she was too upset to remember much of anything about it. Next thing she knew, she was trussed up hand and foot, and gagged with an old towel, and laying in her bathtub.

"The Bronsons had new plumbing put in only last summer. Mighty proud of their bathroom; there's only two others in Fast Harbor! Well, that devil wasn't satisfied with knockin' her senseless, and then going through all her closets and bureaus and stealing what little money and jewelry he could find, but he'd left her helpless in the tub, flat on her back, and turned on the cold water faucet. He'd put in the plug, and when she come to the water had already riz high enough to reach her shoulders. It was only a matter of minutes when it'd reach her mouth and nose and drowned her! Somehow, she herself don't know how she done it, she managed to work herself loose, just in time, and set up. Then she fainted; and when she came to again, the tub was full and runnin' over. She says it's gone through the floor and spoiled the kitchen ceiling," finished Neighbor Hodge, with an anticlimax of which he was unconscious.

"Haven't they any idea who did it?" asked Weston, his teeth chattering a little. "Seems as if she'd recognize something familiar about the assailant. You all must know one another pretty well around here!"

"She's sure he don't belong in these parts," Hodge said. "And so far he hasn't been caught up with. Of course, they're out looking for him. Tomorrow soon as it gits light enough, they'll try to track him. But anyhow, he's got clear away. Bronson come home about an hour after his wife got herself free, and he telephoned right to the sheriff in Allsworth, and it was him notified me. And I dressed myself and come right on over to warn ye folks. It ain't likely he'll trouble you none; but you never can tell. Crazy, I says. No professional burglar would bother to do such a thing, when the woman was already helpless and he'd got all there was lying loose. Took about eleven dollars, and Mrs. Bronson's best silver spoons and forks, and a string of gold beads that belonged to her grandmother. That's all they've missed, so far."

Jason Hodge turned aside, as if to go. Weston recollected himself, and stepped to one side. "Won't you come in, and let my wife make you a cup of tea or something? I'm sure we are very grateful to you, and sorry for your trouble!"

Hodge shook his head. "Nope. Never drink tea late at night, much obliged. And as for the trouble, we folks out in the country always aim to be neighborly. Not like the city, where I've heard it said the dwellers in the same tenements live on for years without even having a bowing acquaintance, nor 'tending one another's funerals! We ain't like that, down here. Only a few of us, and we try to act human."

Weston laughed. "That slam was deserved, I guess, Mr. Hodge! We do get sort of inhuman in the big cities. But that's partly because families are always coming and going; and in emergencies there are always policemen and doctors to be had at a moment's notice. But I certainly do thank you, and I'll sleep with one eye open. If I can help track down the robber tomorrow, call on me! I want to do my share, too."

Hodge was already moving down the path toward the gate. He turned and spoke over his shoulder. "Guess it'll take somebody who can read signs to do that, mister! Somebody that knows the woods. A man could hide out for weeks in these deep cedar swamps. Pretty thinly settled! But we'll root the varmint out, if he's anywheres about. And when we ketch him, he'll be lucky if he ever lives to be tried!"

A moment later the gate clicked in the darkness, and Weston rebolted his door. He also went over the rooms on the lower floor, closed and locked each window. He had bolted his door through sheer habit; all the windows had been left open, for the fresh air. They were screened against mosquitoes, but otherwise unprotected. He turned and mounted the stairs, to find Annie standing shivering on the top landing.

"How perfectly awful!" she exclaimed, "I heard all he said. And we supposed that up here we'd get away from all the lawlessness and assaults and murders and things our city papers are full of! I didn't dream any worse crime was ever heard of up here in this lovely country than the theft of a watermelon, or the bootlegging of a little hard cider by some thrifty farmer! Oh, Frank, I don't believe I'm going to like it here. Let's go to some civilized resort, and give up our rental here!"

Weston put a reassuring arm across her shoulder and gently urged her back to her room.

"Shucks! Wait till tomorrow, and see how different you feel in

the bright sunshine. I don't believe there are any dangerous people living within twenty miles of us. This was the act of some tramp crazy with hooch, or dope. They'll catch him; and nothing exciting will happen here again for fifty years more. But isn't it queer that this should occur the very night we arrived to enjoy the simple life!"

Contrary to their expectations, both fell asleep within fifteen minutes, nor were they troubled with bad dreams. They were roused only when Romeo, the bobtailed cat, scandalized at the idea of lying abed after the sun was up, perched on Weston's pillow and patted his face with imperative paws. He opened his eyes, grinned, and called out to Annie that it was a grand morning, and that he could do with a bit of breakfast!

As Weston had prophesied, his wife felt differently about their new home in the bright morning sunshine. Robins and bluebirds were singing, and selecting home sites. Down on the shore, crows were strutting up and down, their sharp beaks attacking periwinkles and mussels. The island of Mt. Desert stood out so clearly that one could make out automobiles crawling up its steep mountain roads. In the lilac bush at the corner of the kitchen, a peabody bird lighted and uttered its joyous song, which our northern cousins insist is a repetition of the word: "Canada."

Annie sang too, as she wrestled with coffee, ham and eggs and toast, all at one time on her stove aflame with seasoned kindling. Frank surveyed his bristly chin in the mirror of his bureau, grinned, and decided not to shave that day. That was one of the petty tyrannies he had come up here to escape! No, and he wouldn't wear any necktie, either. Just a flannel shirt open at the neck, the new corduroy trousers, and on his feet a pair of easy buckskin shoes. Bareheaded, he would wander about and get the lay of the land after breakfast. He too sang, discordantly, but none the less happily.

But before breakfast was fairly over, they had a caller, two of them, in fact; one remained outside, at the wheel of the stanch old touring car. The other, a determined-looking man with a square chin and sea-blue eyes, a man in his vigorous fifties and wearing loose blue serge and a slouch hat, knocked at the door. By daylight, there was nothing ominous about this knocking; it didn't seem nearly as loud as the summons of Jason Hodge in the blackness of night.

He nodded at Frank as he answered the door, a piece of buttered toast in one hand and toast crumbs sprinkling his flannel shirt.

"Mr. Weston? From New York? Thought so. I'm Thomas, Joe Thomas from Allsworth—sheriff. Suppose you've heard about what happened last night?"

"Hodge came over to tell me," Weston said. "He knew we have no telephone. Won't you come in, Mr. Thomas? We can rustle up a cup of hot coffee—"

The sheriff interrupted him with a gesture of one hand.

"Much obliged; but this is my busy day. What time did Jason tell you about what happened at Bronson's place?"

"Why—I don't know exactly; I think I'd just fallen asleep, and we retired about ten o'clock. Couldn't have been much later than ten thirty."

"Then you really don't know what all could have taken place afterward."

"Why, no. We locked up tight, and then went to sleep again; and you're the first one I've seen since I talked with Hodge."

The sheriff nodded. "Just so. Well, there was another outrage along toward three o'clock. Same fellow, apparently; anyhow he was masked, and he had plenty of time to walk over to old man Tucker's cabin. That's beyond Cranberry Beach a few miles; nearest neighbor is a mile away. Tucker has always had the reputation of being a miser. I don't know why; I doubt if he's got ten dollars to his name. But anyhow, this bandit—whoever it was—broke into his shack, woke up the old man and tried to make him tell where his money was hid. Didn't get nothing out of him. Not even when he tied him up and held lighted matches to the soles of his feet and did other devilish things I haven't time to go into now. He left along about half past four, as well as Tucker can figure out. The poor old codger is in a bad way. They took him over to Allsworth, to the hospital. He's hurt, some; but the shock to his nerves is worse, the doctors say. So, you see Hodge's warning isn't one to be taken lightly."

Weston was genuinely shocked. Coming as he had from a city where atrocious crimes were the familiar headlines of his breakfast paper, he had expected to forget such things in the peaceful country of scattered farms, deep woods, and majestic ocean. They seemed worse, somehow, these brutal assaults, than they had back home. They seemed to desecrate the loveliness of nature; to make the bird songs and the fleecy clouds and warm sunshine a mockery.

He was seeking to find some expression of his feelings when Thomas spoke again.

"Just you and your wife here? So I understood. And you got in—when?"

"Yesterday, about four o'clock. Jed Hooper drove us over from Cherryville Junction in his car. We came up on the Down-Easter through train from New York."

"Strangers here, I take it? How'd you come to learn about the place?"

Weston smiled. "I picked out about the location we desired, on a road map. Then I wrote the postmaster at Cherryville, and he sent me a number of names; Hooper's was among them. So then I wrote him, and from his description I engaged the Jarvis house."

He looked the sheriff steadily and a trifle quizzically in the eyes. "I guess you're asking me to establish a sort of alibi, Mr. Thomas?"

The sheriff reddened slightly, then laughed. "There isn't a chance in the world that you had anything to do with these two affairs, Weston. But one of the things I have to do is check up on every man, woman and grown child who lives hereabout and could by any chance, however remote, have been to the Bronson and Tucker places last night. That's dry detail; but it has to be attended to, or I'll get what-for from the district attorney!"

He turned to go; then paused for a final word.

"Don't let this fret you and the missus too much. We're bound to get that murdering dog. I've got men that know every mile of this district like it was their own woodpile. Besides which, the roads will be patrolled. I'm swearing in deputies today. You'll see some of 'em before sundown. And if you hear or see anything suspicious, no matter how trivial it seems to you, be sure to notify one of my men right off. G'bye!"

Weston watched until he swung himself into the waiting car, and was driven rapidly down the sandy road towards Hooper's place.

"That was the sheriff," he explained to Annie when he returned to the kitchen for a final cup of coffee. "There was another holdup last night—an old man miles away up the beach somewhere. Nobody was killed or seriously hurt. And before night there'll be someone on guard along the highway. If they don't catch the fellow, they'll at least make it too dangerous for him to attempt anything further around here."

Annie tried to believe him; her common sense argued that he was right. But somehow, the warmth seemed to have gone from the sunshine. And the birds seemed to have stopped their song, this was natural enough, as their early chorus was over, and they were busy about their affairs. Only Romeo, the bobtailed cat, seemed oblivions of the dark cloud that had descended over the peaceful little hamlet of Fast Harbor. Promptly after he had lapped up his saucer of warm milk, he wandered forth to investigate the life and habits of the field mouse, as found in his dooryard.

When Weston would have imitated his cat to the extent of strolling away from the house, Annie entered a terrified protest.

"Where are you going with that pail, Frank?" she cried. To his reply that he was thinking of going down to the beach which lay just beyond a clump of cedars, to see if he could dig some clams, she objected: "But there's nearly a peck of clams from those Mr. Hooper left here for us!"

He hesitated, glancing longingly at the short iron clam hook in his hand, "Well, I thought it would be rather good fun. And they will keep indefinitely, if I leave a little water in the pail and sprinkle some corn meal over them. I read that in a newspaper."

Annie's voice was a little sharp with terror as she answered him. "Yes, and first thing you know, you'll be reading in a newspaper that Mrs. Frank Weston was found murdered in her summer camp, while her husband was amusing himself on the shore!"

Half vexed and half amused, he yielded. "If I've got to stick around the dooryard all the time, we might as well pull stakes and go to a hotel. One reason for coming up here was to get a lot of exercise and fresh air! If you're worried, and I don't wonder, why not put on your old shoes and come along with me?"

She shook her head, "No; I've got my housework to attend to. Beds to make, dinner to get started. Of course we'll take walks all about the country together; but not right after breakfast. You said there'd be some guards posted nearby, didn't you?"

"So the sheriff promised. All right, then. I'll wait till they show up before I go out of sight of the house."

He reluctantly set down his pail and clam hook, and pottered about the rough dooryard, pulling clumps of weeds, removing loose stones from the driveway, working up an appetite by splitting some kindling, although Jed Hooper had prepared a generous supply of fuel in advance

of their coming.

The day dragged monotonously. Weston missed his daily papers and the mail he always looked over before going to his office. He hated to admit it, but he even missed the noise and bustle of the city, the throbbing of industry and pleasure and all that went to make up the ordered confusion of a metropolis. Nobody passed the house; lacking a telephone, he could not call up to inquire what progress, if any, had been made toward capturing the murderous unknown.

But directly after dinner, which they ate in an abstracted silence, big Jason Hodge appeared. He was leading a miserable-looking cur, whose pedigree would have puzzled a dog fancier. He hailed Weston with rough cordiality.

"Brought ye a watchdog! He ain't much to look at, but he sure does make a row if he hears anybody prowling about the house. Thought the missus would feel easier at night with him tied up outside. If you don't hear Tige yellin', you can rest easy there's nobody sneaking up on ye in the dark. Keep him till we've caught the miscreant."

"Mighty good of you," Weston thanked him, eyeing the dog dubiously. "Then I take it nothing has been found yet? No clues?"

"There's a posse out now beating up the woods and swamps. Soon as I learn anything I'll come right over and tell you."

He looked about, selected a juniper bush whose scrubby boughs formed a shelter close to the ground, dragged the slinking mongrel to it and made fast his rope. "He don't need no kennel this warm weather," he explained. "Just feed him twice a day; any scraps left over from the table. Tige ain't particular. And see that he has plenty of water. Soon as we catch our man, I'll come over and fetch him home."

Weston thanked him as cordially as he was able, the dog circled his tree two or three times, winding himself up in his rope, then sniffed resignedly and laid himself down on the sunny side and went to sleep. Hodge strode with long-legged steps back toward his farm, and life at the old Jarvis place went on as before.

The westering sun was sending the long, thin shadows of the cedars and spruces across the yard when two strange men heaved in sight from up the road.

There was something grim and businesslike about their look, dressed as they were in rough shooting coats, with breeches tucked into their boots, and rifles under their arms. One of them turned in through the gate and approached Weston, who was feeding the guardian dog.

"Seen any strangers about?" he asked.

Weston shook his head. "You are all strangers to me; all but the sheriff, Hodge and Hooper. But nobody else has been near us; or at least, I have seen no one. You one of the guards Thomas spoke of?"

"That's me. Name of Larkin. I trap, winters, and do a little lobstering summers. Got a string of pots out in the cove now. Thomas told me to take over a mile or two of the road about here. Nights, that means. Don't allow there'll be any daylight assaults."

"Well, that's certainly fine! And if you want anything, don't hesitate to call on us. My wife will be glad to get up in the middle of the night and make you a cup of coffee, or rustle a lunch."

Larkin grinned. "I've tromped the wilderness too long to pamper myself that way, mister! My own wife sees to it I start out with a full stomach, and I've more'n once hit the trail for two days with no more than a handful of crackers and a drink of melted snow. But if you see or hear anything unusual, tip me off, will you? The selectmen have offered a reward for the capture, and I could use it."

Twice that night, Weston rose from his bed and peered out into the darkness; and once he made out the shadowy figure of Larkin as he stole cautiously down the road, making no more noise than an Indian, and keeping to the edge of the road where the cedars cast a protecting gloom.

Neither Frank nor his wife slept well, although greatly eased in their minds by the presence of alert watchers, armed to kill. It was Jason Hodge's dog which was responsible for their insomnia. Every little while he broke into astonishing howls and ululations, sounds that it did not seem as if his wizened body could give voice to. The animal was uneasy in a strange place, irked by being tied up, and doubtless aware of the passing guards. There was less reassurance in his warning bark than there was annoyance to the would-be sleepers, Both were tired and irritable when they sat down for breakfast next morning; and Annie insisted that the dog be led back to its owner that very day.

"Every time he wakes me up I jump a foot!" she declared. "I might as well be murdered, as scared to death!"

Hodge ambled past during the forenoon; and Weston returned the dog with thanks and explanations.

"He keeps my wife awake with his howling. And now that there are guards posted—man named Larkin has this section to cover—we don't really need the dog."

Hodge nodded understandingly.

"Guess that's right. Tige would warn ye if the bandit come near; but he's bound to make just as much fuss over a passing guard, or a rabbit, or a skunk. He means well, but he talks too much. If he wan't such a good coon dog, I'd shoot him. He's spoiled a deal of sleep for me, too!"

CHAPTER III
A STRANGER

Before dusk fell that afternoon, there was plenty of evidence that the countryside was astir. Where hitherto there had been almost complete isolation, the road was now alive with men on foot, in rackety secondhand cars, and on horseback. Here and there an expensive make of automobile drove past, filled with those whom curiosity had drawn from Allsworth, and even as far away as Bangor. There were reporters and camera men among the rest. The sandy highway began to take on the aspects of a thriving town street.

Weston reflected that almost any one of the men who straggled past, some of them pausing to gape at him as he lounged smoking a pipe in his doorway, might be the murderous bandit who had strangely enough chosen this quiet, law-abiding and by no means wealthy neck of the woods for his assaults and depredations. They were all strangers to him, save the three or four men and one woman he had come to know. But there was comfort in their very numbers; and although toward twilight they thinned out, and finally disappeared save for the solemnly parading sentry, Larkin, Weston and Annie both retired that night without any fears. They were careful to lock everything fast downstairs, and the loaded automatic rested under Frank's pillow. He wished that he might practice with it a little; but the sound of shots would certainly bring a lot of excited and inquisitive men to their little house. He believed that he had mastered the mechanism, and that he wouldn't in an emergency forget to slip the safety catch. But there wouldn't be any emergency; of this he felt sure. With morning, word would probably come that the bandit had been captured.

Instead of which, morning brought Jed Hooper and his wife, Lizzie, with news of a fresh outrage. The masked man, eluding all the trackers, had broken into an unoccupied summer cottage five miles down the shore, ransacking it. The owner had been notified; until he arrived, it was impossible to say just how much had been stolen. Lacking any human victim, the bandit had sated his bad temper on the furnishings. A costly radio set had been wrecked; rugs and pictures were slashed, glass and china broken.

"Course, we don't know for sure that it's the same man," Hooper admitted, "but it's reasonable to s'pose it is. 'Tain't likely there's two sech wild men runnin' loose about Fast Harbor! He's a loony, says I, and cunning as a weasel, like crazy folk is apt to be. A criminal lunatic. Sheriff Thomas has found some faint footprints at two of the places, and measured 'em; but that don't amount to nothing till we find some shoes to fit 'em to—and some feet in the shoes! It looks like he hid out in the cottage a night or two. One of the beds has been slept in, and some tinned grub opened, and water boiled on an oil stove."

"If you folks are nervous," Lizzie invited, "you're more'n welcome to come over and stop with us till they catch him. You'd feel easier where there's four of us, than just you two, being as you're strangers here. There's plenty of room, and folks say they never get up hungry from my table!"

"That is awfully dear of you, Mrs. Hooper; but truly, Frank and I are not alarmed. He has his revolver ready, and we are careful about our doors and windows. Nobody could get in without making a lot of noise, and Frank will give them a warm welcome! Besides, Larkin is on guard near by; and soon as he heard a shot he'd hurry to us with his rifle."

"Well, that's sensible," Lizzie Hooper agreed. "But I didn't know just how you'd feel about it, and wanted you to know we feel sort of responsible for getting you up here, where you expected to have a good rest!"

The good woman stayed for an hour or so and helped Annie with advice about certain details of cooking; and Frank chatted pleasantly enough with Jed, over a couple of mugs of the smooth cider from the keg in the cellar. There was less passing along the road, today; but quite a number had been identified by Jed during his call, and there were others who were strangers to him.

"I reckon I know by sight every man within fifteen mile," he declared. "So there must be some who have come from quite a ways off. Cats ain't all the critters that are pestered by curiosity! Well, we got into the city papers, anyhow; Portland, and even Boston. Your name's mentioned, too. 'Mr.

Frank Weston and wife, of Riverside Drive, New York, are summering in Fast Harbor, which is just now the center of an unknown bandit's activities.' That's what it said; I memorized it to tell ye."

Weston laughed. "I don't know as this sort of publicity does any of us much good!"

Hooper pondered over this. "I've heard say that it don't matter so much what they say about ye, if only they say something!"

"That has been the motto of some famous characters," Weston admitted. "Anyhow, the more publicity, the harder it will be for the bandit to escape capture. There must be a hundred men looking for him, right now."

"We're a leetle mite slow getting started," Jed said. "But the whole county will be on his trail before the week's out. The reward will fetch him, I know I could use that five hundred easy! And so could a lot of others. Guess likely you're the only resident that don't need it."

After the Hoopers had left, and with the potatoes boiling for dinner, Annie joined her husband, sitting beside him on the doorstep. There seemed nothing better to do than to watch the passersby. But of these, there seemed only a scattered few. There was nothing to attract them to this particular spot; those who passed were on their way to the Bronson house or old man Tucker's shack, or the looted cottage. And by noon, the road was as deserted as usual. Larkin wouldn't come on till dark.

Suddenly, and without warning, a small gray body hurtled between them, shot out into the yard, and made for a clump of junipers. It was Romeo, his hair erect, whiskers twitching, and spitting as he went. His tail would have been ruffed up had it been anything but the mere stump it was!

Weston's pipe had dropped from his surprised lips. Annie screamed a little, then laughed. "Well, what do you know about that! He was asleep by the kitchen stove when I came out. What do you suppose—"

Her words died away as a slight noise from the rear of the house caught her ear. She rose and turned toward the kitchen.

"Wait! Let me go first," Frank cried; and thrusting her aside almost brusquely, he hurried through the living room and into the kitchen. At the door, he paused uncertainly. A man—a stranger—stood in the middle of the floor, regarding him with a faint grin.

He was a slightly built, pleasant-faced man of about thirty-five, dressed neatly and almost fastidiously in well-fitting clothes, and wearing a pearl-gray felt hat which he removed as he caught sight of Weston's wife standing at his shoulder. He set down a small traveling bag as he spoke.

"I knocked, but I fancy you didn't hear me."

His voice was agreeable and low pitched. "And I seem to have scared your cat into a fit! Sorry."

"What did you do to Romeo?" Annie asked, her courage returning

"Not a thing, I assure you! The truth is, cats sort of have it in for me. I rather like them; but they don't reciprocate. Down at the office they poke a lot of fun at me about it. But let me introduce myself properly."

From an inside breast pocket he look a black leather case, and from it removed a business card which he handed to Weston It read: "Sanford Teller, Detective. Representing the Wallis Detective Agency. Boston."

"I may also add that I have full credentials in this pocket case, and a real, shiny new badge," the stranger added. In proof of the latter assertion he unbuttoned the top of his vest and showed on the under side an oval silver shield, bearing the title of detective and a number.

"Well, I declare!" said Annie. "You don't look one bit like a detective! Of course, I never saw one before, to know him."

Mr. Teller bowed gracefully. "You flatter me, madam! The one man I don't want to look like is a detective. And so, your words are balm to my spirit."

He turned to Weston. "Your name I know. I read of your arrival in a Boston daily; and I already knew more or less of your financial position in New York. Now, Mr. Weston, it is urgent that I have a few words in private with you. Will Mrs. Weston think me too rude, if—"

Annie colored slightly. "Certainly not! But if you two will use one of the front rooms, I'll finish getting dinner ready. For after all, this is my domain, Mr. Teller!"

The urbane sleuth bowed gallantly. "Granted, Mrs. Weston! And I'll explain to your husband how I came to call at the back door, instead of the front. And he has my permission to tell you as much as he chooses, of what I tell him."

He stooped over and picked up his grip, and followed his host to the front of the house, while Annie gingerly stuck a fork into one of the bubbling potatoes, as Lizzie Hooper had told her to do. She wasn't at all sure whether they were done or not; the fork seemed to go in easily enough. She set them farther back on the stove, and began to cut thin slices from a ham.

The two men meanwhile had seated themselves in the parlor, a room the Westons had not had any occasion to use so far. To Weston's suggestion that they sit on the doorstep, the detective objected. Not only that, but he carefully closed the door, and took pains to sit far back in the room, out of range of the window.

"All this seems very mysterious, and stagy," he said. "But it is dictated by strict common sense. I am afraid your well-earned privacy is about to be invaded, sir! Almost overnight your little village has become unhappily notorious. And that is why I am here."

He leaned forward, his quiet voice pitched still lower.

"I have been lurking in the cedar grove behind your house for half an hour," he confessed. "When I was as certain as I could be that the coast was clear, I hustled across the backyard; and when you didn't answer my knock, I didn't waste a moment. It may have been impolite, but I simply came right on in!"

Once more he took out his pocket case, glanced over a number of papers, selected one. "Here is a copy, on our official paper, of a letter received by Mr. Wallis—my employer—from the assistant district attorney, Mr. Frothingham. You will note that he requests that an agent be sent as soon as possible from Boston. The truth is, Mr. Weston, that the district attorney knows as well as I do—and as you probably do —that this case is a little out of the ordinary experience of country constables! While Thomas, the sheriff, is a good man as far as he goes, shrewd and energetic, he has never handled anything more intricate than chasing down an illicit still, or helping the fish warden stop the destruction of short lobsters, or lock up the village cut-up occasionally. Something a little more up-to-date than the hick constable is needed right now, and that is why I am here. Got in this morning, early, and have kept out of sight.

"My experience has been almost entirely with bank men and loft workers in the cities; and the only reason for sending me up here is that I was pretty familiar with the country, because as a boy my father used to rent a summer place at Bar Harbor year after year. I've hunted and fished for miles up and down the coast."

"But just why have you called on me?" Weston asked. "I'm probably the one man within twenty miles who is least fitted to give you the slightest information or advice! We have only just moved in, and were never here before."

Teller smiled, fished in his pockets again, and this time took out a handsome pigskin cigar case. He offered it to Weston, who accepted a panatela. Teller held the match, lighted one himself. When it was drawing, he spoke again.

"You've answered your own question! The one thing I don't want is advice, or alleged information! And I'd be swamped with it if I were to approach anybody else. They're great gossips in these parts; and just now, everybody is bursting with theories and rumors. It is vital for my success, that my presence be not so much as suspected. At my suggestion, Mr. Wallis wrote the district attorney not to notify Sheriff Thomas, or any one else, that our agency is interested in the case. We work alone, sir, and in the dark. And now I come to the gist of the matter. The truth is, and much as I regret to do so, I am obliged to make an awkward request, the decision on which must, of course, rest with you and Mrs. Weston. If I am to work in secret, my presence unsuspected by the local police, and my work unhampered, *where am I going to stay?* And here is where you come in, if you will!"

Weston looked startled. "You mean, you want to stay *here*? To eat and sleep in this house?"

Teller nodded and blew a beautiful smoke ring.

"Sounds nervy, doesn't it? Of course I needn't say that you may send the Wallis Agency a bill in full, and you don't need to be too modest about the amount, either! This county is paying all the expenses. But I also realize that is isn't a question of money, but the interruption of what was intended to be a restful, quiet vacation. Well, as to that, let me remind you that this rest and quiet has already been somewhat upset by the events of the past two nights. And furthermore, I shall be here only by day. I must got some sleep and have a place in which to hide out, and make my reports to Wallis. As soon as it is dark, I shall be off on my investigations. I am as good as a cat for seeing in the dark! Maybe that is one reason why cats dislike me. We are rival night prowlers, in the estimation of puss! But joking aside, I should sleep forenoons, require only the plainest of food, and not much of that; work at my reports and the assembling of any clues I may dig up through the afternoon, and be off and away as soon as night falls.

"Forget me; think only of your duty as a citizen. This law-abiding little community is terrorized by a nameless peril. The chances are ten to one against its solution by the local constabulary. The chances are about that in my favor; I have a pretty good record for getting my men! But in order to work unhampered, I must have a hangout. All I need is a shake down and a blanket; I'm used to roughing it. That, and some food."

Weston pondered for some moments, his brow furrowed. Then it cleared, and he spoke up. "Of course, Teller, I can't decide a thing like this without speaking to my wife!"

"By all means! I wouldn't stay here for a moment unless she sanctioned it. Be perfectly frank with her. I trust you both."

Frank went back to the kitchen, where the ham was already sizzling, and a bowl of fresh eggs stood ready to be dropped into the hot fat. Briefly he told Annie the situation as Teller had outlined it. Rather to his relief, she insisted that the detective must be sheltered.

"Aside from it being our plain duty," she said as she turned a slice of ham without spattering too much hot grease, "think what a protection he will be! You can have your walks, and dig clams, and fish or anything, because he will be here all day. Then at night, you will be home. I'll have a big, strong man at hand to protect me twenty-four hours a day! And now, ask him to have dinner with us. It will be ready in a jiffy."

It was a jolly meal, even though Romeo sulked and would not come inside for his food, which had to be set outside the door for him. To both Weston and his wife, it was quite an experience to talk familiarly with a real detective. They had read many mystery stories, but never before had they seen a detective; they might have, of course, but at least they had not recognized him as one. And the Wallis Agency was internationally known. It never handled any dirty cases; and it frequently cooperated with the police of many cities, and even of countries abroad. Wallis, the founder, had at one time been a Boston police chief.

Teller laughingly refused to discuss the present case.

"I only just arrived, and I don't allow myself to do any theorizing until I've looked over the ground. But I promise you this: you are my partners now, and whatever I learn, I'll disclose to you. We will work the case over together. It happens more often than you think, that an outsider, one with no connection whatever with the forces of law and order, furnishes us professionals with a priceless suggestion! You are a sound business man, sir, and I grant Mrs. Weston a full share of woman's intuition!"

Teller slept for quite a while after dinner. His long night journey, taken at such short notice that he had been unable to obtain a sleeping berth, had tired him. Toward dusk, he awakened, and had supper with them; but he seemed preoccupied with the hour drawing near when he must set forth on the hunt for clews.

Annie had fixed up a comfortable cot for him on the sofa in the parlor; at his request, the blinds were drawn, all the windows closed. He placed his grip in a little cupboard, and carefully removed all traces of his presence.

"Not a word to the sheriff, if he calls, nor to anyone else!" he warned, "You won't have to lie, for nobody suspects my presence, and nobody but the district attorney knows that we are in on the case at all. I have made arrangements to communicate with him, and to forward my reports to Boston."

Shortly after darkness had fallen, Sanford Teller, with the furtiveness that delighted Annie as the proper attitude of a sleuth, crept from the house by the kitchen door, and after peering up and down for some moments, darted across the strip of rough ground and was lost to sight in the cedar grove.

"It isn't the simple life we expected, but isn't it just too thrilling?" Annie chattered as they climbed the narrow stairway to their chambers. "Like one of these mystery plays, only lots more real!"

CHAPTER IV
GOLD BEADS

Annie was awakened by a sunbeam which found its way in through a chink in the blinds and struck her full in the eye. Her first thought was of their strange guest.

"Good gracious! And he wanted to get into the house unseen. We never thought to leave the kitchen door unlocked, nor to give him the key!"

She hastily threw on a loose robe, and pattered into the front room where her husband still slept. She shook his shoulder impatiently, and as his eyes opened lazily, she cried: "Oh, Frank! That poor Mr. Teller must be hiding out in the cedar grove, waiting for us to let him in!"

But the resourceful Teller was doing nothing of the sort. When Weston had hastily donned some clothes and slipped downstairs, he heard through the parlor door the deep respirations of a sleeping

man; and, cautiously peering within, he beheld the detective reposing on his couch, the blanket drawn up to his eyebrows. Leaving him in peace, Weston passed on to the kitchen and tried the door. It was locked; as were all the windows. Returning to the upper floor, he told Annie what he had found.

Both now dressed fully, and Annie set the coffeepot on and got out the eggs and began to toast bread. Weston meanwhile knocked at the parlor door. And at the first tap of his knuckles, Sanford Teller sat abruptly up in his bed, his eyes wide awake and alert. Weston grinned.

"We were afraid we'd locked you out, and overslept! How on earth did you manage to get in?"

Teller laughed cheerily, and rose in a pair of sky-blue pajamas, stretching his arms luxuriously. "Getting into locked houses is the easiest part of my profession, Weston! Truth is, we have a lot of tricks in common with crooks. I forgot to speak about leaving the kitchen key where I could find it when I returned about half past three; but that didn't matter. I judge that I didn't disturb you or Mrs. Weston when I came in and very quietly went to bed?"

"No, but you disturbed her when she awoke and remembered that you wanted to come back here in the dark, before any one passing by could see you! You hurry up and get washed and dressed; breakfast is 'most ready. And while we're eating it you can tell her how you managed to get in."

Teller grinned. "I don't know about that! It don't do to tell too much. Got to hold some things back, or there won't be anything mysterious about me. And that would be fatal to the reputation of a detective, you know!"

But under the mellow influence of hot coffee and fresh-boiled eggs and buttered toast that wasn't burned the least little bit, he yielded, and showed them a long, slim skeleton key, one of a bunch he kept on a ring.

"There are probably some doors and drawers in this county that this collection wouldn't open," he admitted. "But I doubt if there are any in Fast Harbor! Better watch out for your spoons and jewelry, Mrs. Weston!"

"The spoons go with the house, and are guaranteed to be silver plated," Annie assured him. "And as for jewelry, you'll have to go to New York and pick the lock in my safety-deposit box to get that. Unless my wedding ring tempts you."

Teller bowed gallantly. "Only to the extent of wishing it might have been given to you by me, madam!"

"Why, how perfectly sweet of you! Frank never says such nice things to me."

"No, but Frank bought the wedding ring!" her

husband reminded her.

It was a cheerful meal and, after it was finished, Teller insisted that it had waked him up so thoroughly that he didn't feel inclined to finish his nap, which he would postpone until later in the day.

When the dishes were done, they gathered about the table in the parlor, careful to keep the windows shut. Weston himself sat where, through a crack in the blinds, he could observe any one approaching the house.

"Of course, I haven't anything to report as yet," Teller stated. "I devoted last night to looking over the sites where the crimes took place. And let me tell you, the woods were swarming with amateur detectives! Everybody but the bedridden—that is, every man—in this neck of the woods is out for that five hundred dollars' reward! Some carry lanterns, a few have pocket torches, and one or two of the local constables go without any lights at all; they are the only ones that worried me. They really do know a lot about tracking; they don't make much noise as they move about, and most of them can shoot fast and straight. But I managed to get what I wanted without being seen or heard; although once or twice I almost brushed elbows with some silent patrol."

He spread out on the table a large road map of the country. Taking from his vest pocket a soft red pencil, he began to mark certain crosses and arrows and lines upon the map.

"Here, you will note, is the location of the Bronson place; and this, a few miles beyond Cranberry Beach, is old Tucker's cabin. Here is the cottage that was broken into; nobody living there, you remember. It was while scouting about it that I had my narrowest escape. Cautious as I was, some guard must have caught a glimpse of me; anyhow, first thing I knew a gunshot raised the hair on my head! Buckshot, the fellow was using; it pattered onto the cottage wall not a foot above my head. I was scared stiff, but not hurt. Dropped flat, and crawled off to a great lilac bush, and from there gained the road. I never saw the man who shot at me, but could hear him thrashing about hunting for me."

Annie drew her breath sharply. "But you run terrible risks! Wouldn't it be better to let the sheriff know who you are, rather than be killed through an error?"

The little man shook his head

vigorously. "That's a risk I've got to take. It's all in the day's work, or rather, the night's work! Once I am known, my usefulness ends. Everybody will be tagging me about, and the criminal will know I am coming a mile before I'm in sight, Might as well hire a brass band to accompany me! No, my only chance of capturing lies in my remaining incognito. But, look!"

He pointed to the map. "By setting down every single site connected with the crimes, we get the first necessary layout of the field of battle. This map, revised from day to day, shows the precise range of the bandit's activities. This is the sort of thing the postal agents work out when there is an epidemic of stolen mail. Every time a loss is reported, a mark is made on the map; and in time, by an intricate system of geometrical cross-lines, we manage to locate the headquarters of the gang. That is something I hope to do with this lone ruffian, if he remains undetected long enough to commit a series of crimes."

He refolded the map, and pocketed it.

"And that is absolutely all I have to tell you," he said. "Can't expect definite results the first night! This sort of chase is likely to prove a long, stern one. But I don't mind telling you this purely theoretical notion of mine: when found, the bandit will prove to me a man known to a good many residents hereabouts. You see, it is always hard for us to believe that anybody we have known well and for a long time, is an actual criminal. We may detest him, admit that he is mean, selfish, unpopular, a tax evader, even a chicken thief, but a murderer? No! Because the very instinct of self-preservation keeps us from admitting that we could possibly live within sight of the home of a murderer!"

"You mean," Weston asked, "that this bandit actually lives within sight of where we are?"

"Not quite that; but I do feel that the perfectly natural instinct of attributing any atrocious crime to a stranger, somebody from far away, is not to be trusted too far. Without hampering myself by any preconceived ideas, I shall, among other things, scrutinize our neighbors pretty closely. Who had the best opportunity to terrorize the Bronson woman, and old Tucker? Who knew that the summer cottage down the shore was unoccupied? Who knows the wilderness about here well enough to so far evade trained guides? Who is able to hide out and obtain food without being detected? Certainly, no stranger, who would be lost within half an hour of the time he entered the great cedar swamp! And more certainly yet, no city-bred man. No, I shall make it one of my first duties to look over the local peasantry! Some queer characters live in lonesome little hamlets like this. The very isolation preys on their minds; they become abnormal. And everything indicates that the man I am after is not normal; he is the victim of some overwhelming homicidal mania. I hope I am wrong; but I never allow sentiment to interfere with my professional duty."

Nothing of further interest occurred that day, save a brief visit from Sheriff Joe Thomas, who alighted from his car and came to the door for a brief word. He looked worn and drawn, and as if he had sacrificed a lot of sleep.

"Heard or seen anything, Mr. Weston? No? Well, I don't expect you will. Did you happen to hear a gunshot last night? Doubt if it would carry this far; wind was in wrong direction. One of my men thought he saw something moving about the Barnard cottage; the one that was broken into. He was taking no chances, so he let a charge of double-b's at it. Heard nothing, and didn't see anything more. But this morning I found some broken twigs and the faintest impression of foot tracks around the cottage. Ground is hard there, and I couldn't get any impressions. Reckon it might have been some curiosity seeker. Don't think the bandit would be fool enough to return, especially since he had time enough to take anything he wanted the first trip. Must be on my way, now. Sorry your vacation is being knocked galley west this way!"

Sanford Teller had listened to the sheriff with quiet amusement. When he had gone, he emerged from the parlor and spoke.

"Your sheriff would be surprised to learn that the man his deputy tried to pot, is about to sit down to dinner with you and your wife, wouldn't he?"

"He'd be more than surprised," Weston mumbled. "He'd certainly give me a fine bawling-out for not telling him!"

"You'll never be really popular with Thomas," Teller decided. "When I nail my man—if I do—the sheriff will be sore as a pup to think that it was done over his head. But such are the dark and devious ways of the Wallis Agency!"

There followed two highly exciting days for the Westons and indeed for the entire countryside. On two successive nights, fresh outrages occurred. Fortunately, there were no deaths; but this was not owing to any clemency on the part of the marauder. In one case, the chance arrival of a visitor interrupted him as he was tying up a crippled fisherman

and his wife, after laying the former low with a stout chair swung about his head; in the other instance, he waylaid a motorist who had got lost, and run out of gas in an abandoned wood road. This man, who was young and vigorous though unarmed, did not suspect the friendly-appearing stranger who appeared afoot, and paused to inquire if he could be of assistance. However, the stranger without warning struck him a terrible blow on the head with a stout cudgel he was using as a walking stick. Dazed, and unable to put up a fight, the man's pockets were rifled, and when some time toward dawn one of the sheriff's men found him, these were all the details he was able to give. Yes, the man wore a handkerchief about his neck, but it was not used as a mask. And the sudden blow, which had just failed to cause a fracture of the skull, left him in too confused a state to give any clear description of his assailant.

Both of these incidents were recounted to Weston by Jason Hodge, who got them by telephone. Weston detailed them to the keenly interested Teller, who marked them with red crosses on his gradually developing map. Meanwhile, the detective himself had at last something of his own to relate.

Despite the fact that he could let himself in with his skeleton key, and did so noiselessly, promptly going to bed until breakfast time, neither Weston nor his wife was able to sleep well toward dawn. They were on the alert to hear some slight sound indicating the return of the little sleuth. There was something uncanny in lying upstairs wrapped in profound slumber, while this man entered their supposedly impregnable house, and went to bed, without making any noise about it, There was, too, the constant fear lest he be shot by one of the deputies during his nocturnal prowlings. Were this to happen, it would be Weston's unpleasant duty to explain to the authorities who he was, and that he had been harbored by them. Not to speak of Weston's liking for the pleasant, cheery little investigator, he foresaw himself as the center of most unpleasant inquiry and criticism.

But Sanford Teller seemed to bear a charmed life. He passed unscathed through a country thickly dotted with keen men, some of whom were professional guides, and all of whom had abnormally good eyes and ears. And despite his handicap of working alone, and in the night, he was making progress, He had, so he explained to the Westons, accumulated a number of finger prints in and about the various scenes of the outrages. He had found a crimson-stained handkerchief, with an initial, a mile from the Bronson place, and although this so far only indicated to him the route taken by the bandit, he had hopes of gaining more information from it. And most sensational of all, on the evening of the fourth day, just after supper and while he was waiting for darkness to mask his operations, he showed them something that sent the cold shivers up Annie's spine, and even caused the little hairs to stir on the scalp of the more phlegmatic Frank,

"This is graveyard stuff," whispered Teller when they had huddled about his parlor table. "I am really violating my obligations to Wallis in making this find public at all! Of course, I have written it all out fully in my daily report, which I shall mail as usual tonight. But I promised you that, in return for your kindness and hospitality, I would be frank with you; that we should, in a way, work together. So, once more let me warn you how terribly important it is that not a word of this shall get out."

He dove into an inside pocket, and threw upon the table top something that glittered dully in the faint light that crept in through the shuttered windows. Annie touched it gingerly, picked it up and held it to the light. It was a tarnished string of gold beads.

"Why, this is very old!" she cried. "See the size of the beads, and how thin they are worn!"

Teller spoke softly. "It was a string of gold beads, belonging to her grandmother, that was among the things stolen from Mrs. Bronson, wasn't it?"

Weston's voice was sharp and nervous as he asked: "Where did these come from, Teller? Where did you find them?"

Teller smiled bleakly. "These beads were concealed very cunningly in the false drawer of an old writing desk in friend Hodge's house. I took the liberty of entering it last night, while he and his wife were asleep. Little habit of mine, you know, to come and go unannounced!"

Annie gasped. "Why—but— you don't suspect—"

Teller raised a deprecating hand. "Let us not deal with suspicions, Mrs. Weston, but with facts. That is where the beads were. In good time, I expect to have them identified and to show why they were hidden in Hodge's writing desk. Meanwhile, forget that I showed them to you. All I can say now is, the trail grows warmer!"

CHAPTER V
IN THE CELLAR

On the morning following, Frank Weston started out on a longer hike than he had as yet undertaken. Ever since Teller had quartered himself at the old Jarvis place, he had been free to wander about and enjoy himself digging clams, or fishing for cunners, swimming in the bracing Atlantic, or simply taking a brisk walk. Annie no longer felt nervous, if his absences were not prolonged. She felt a little natural apprehension lest he meet up with the desperado in some lonesome spot; but so far he had committed all his outrages in the blackness of night.

On his tramps, Weston always carried his automatic; and when down on the beach, he had practiced with it, shooting at bits of driftwood. Teller also had a gun which he carried loose in the side pocket of his coat. There was no part of the twenty-four hours when Annie was not, as she and Weston both felt, adequately protected.

On this bright morning, Frank purposed to pay a visit to the looted cottage. This was several miles down the shore; and owing to the fact that the shore line was not straight, but wound in and out and was broken by many little estuaries, it took him some three hours to arrive.

There wasn't much to see; a caretaker had been installed, the place had been cleaned up, and a list of the things stolen proved to be not very serious. Nothing of much value save the radio outfit and some good rugs and pictures had been left in the cottage over the winter. The caretaker welcomed him, the time dragging somewhat in this remote place; and he went over the house, but found little to interest him. So, after giving the man a handful of cigars, and thanking him, he started back for home, this time taking to the highway in order to save time and arrive for dinner.

He had proceeded less than half a mile when a swiftly driven touring car passed him. Directly after, it slowed down, and the man who was not driving turned and waved a hand at him.

Sheriff Thomas sat in the tonneau; Frank noticed that his face was grim and unshaven. He opened the door, beckoned. "Can I give you a lift? You're a long way from home!"

"Took a notion to run down and look over the Barnard cottage," Weston explained. "I like to get all the exercise I can these fine days."

Thomas nodded gloomily. "I have some serious news which you probably haven't heard," he said as the driver started on again.

"Another assault?"

"Murder, this time. Just found the body early this morning. It was taken over to Allsworth about an hour ago."

Weston paled. "Who was it? The victim, I mean?"

Thomas nervously rolled the unlighted cigar between his lips. "Man named Teller. Sanford Teller, a Wallis operative."

Weston's mouth opened soundlessly. It was a full moment before he could collect himself enough to speak. When he did so, his voice sounded harsh and dry like a gear that needed oiling. "H-how did you know who it was? Did you find identifying papers on him?"

Thomas turned in his seat, and looked at his passenger in surprise. "Why, no. As a matter of fact, his pockets had been turned inside out. There was nothing identifying on him; I knew who it was because Teller was sent up here to help run down the wild man! Matter of fact, outside of the district attorney and his assistant and myself, nobody knew he was up here at all. I hadn't even told my deputy. He was working along his own lines."

"And you say this—Teller was killed this morning?"

"I did not say so. I said his body was found this morning. The medical examiner stated that he had been dead not less than twenty-four hours."

A darkness seemed to have closed in about Weston. In it his mind groped uncertainly. Not yet could he reason clearly; the nameless terror that stole upon him was still undefined, without logic. When he spoke again, his voice was hardly more than a whisper so that the sheriff had to lean toward him to catch what he said.

"Sanford Teller—the Wallis operative—he has been staying in my house four days; and—"

The unlighted cigar dropped from Thomas' lips. *"What's that?"* he cried sharply. "What are you saying?"

Weston roused himself with an effort, as a drugged man forces himself back to the realities of life. "He said that nobody was to know he had been called in, only the district attorney who sent for him. I was above all not to mention his presence to you. And he had papers, a card and a shield—but this other, the man you knew as Teller, have you really any clue as to who killed—"

Sheriff Thomas took from a pocket a small card

bearing the photograph of a man in three sections, a full front, and two profiles. Below were a few lines of coarse print which danced before Weston's groggy eyes. But the face that he gazed upon was that of the man who had been his guest for the past few days, the man who was even now in the same house with Annie, miles away—

He covered his face with his trembling hands, and called upon God to have mercy upon him, to permit him to arrive in time!

"Can't your man drive faster?" he gasped. "My wife—alone there with—"

The sheriff interrupted him harshly. "With the man whose rogue's gallery photograph I just showed you? And you took him in, and hid him, and never told me—"

"But I just said that he explained that it was imperative that his presence remain a secret! That you—the local police—"

"That we were a lot of hick cops, I suppose," put in Thomas. "That we would fall down on the case, and if we knew he was here would crab his game! Was that it? I thought so! Well, Weston, let me tell you something. While you have been sheltering a dangerous maniac, the hick cops went quietly ahead, got fingerprints, sent them on to Boston, and just got this man's full record. A lifer from the Bedford Asylum for the criminally insane; escaped a month ago; lived only a few miles away from Fast Harbor as a lad, but not under the name he has used since. True, we haven't got him yet; but he can't elude us much longer. No wonder he fooled us, with you sheltering him every night!"

"Days," murmured the stricken Weston. "He never went out till after dark. And he told us what progress he was making. Only this morning showed us a necklace of gold beads—"

"Which he himself stole from the Bronson woman! Just as he stole Teller's credentials after murdering him and concealing his body in the swamp where only by the barest chance it would ever have been found!"

"Don't rub it in, now!" begged Weston. "Just hurry! If only God will let me find Annie alive—"

The harsh lines faded a little from Thomas' face. He shook the other's arm with rough kindliness. "Pull yourself together, man! He's far too cunning to touch her. Why, you're the best bet he has! Safe and snug at your place, he can sneak out nights and rob and assault and murder to his heart's content. And we are already driving twice as fast as it's safe to do."

After a moment he added: "I must say, though, that you haven't shown that sound judgment I gave you credit for! I'm a countryman, and there's a lot about crooks that I don't know. But after all, I'm sheriff of this county, and in full charge. Wallis wouldn't dream of sending an operative up here without having him report to me. The fact that he didn't report either to me or to headquarters yesterday, worried me; and my men have been looking for Teller as much as they have for Schmidt. That's what your man calls himself when he is among friends."

Weston had no heart for a reply. What a cursed fool he had been! To swallow the story of a lunatic, and to aid and abet him at the very time he was carrying on his reign of terror! That story about finding the gold beads in Jason Hodge's house; why, anybody with the slightest ability to estimate character would know that Jason was the salt of the earth! While Teller—Schmidt—he was too smooth, too plausible. At that, he seemed more the type who went in for phony stock promotions than for red-handed murder! Probably these spells came on him from time to time; perhaps between his outbreaks he was perfectly normal; didn't even recall them! But Frank was in a state of frenzy meantime; for, suppose one of the attacks of homicidal mania would seize him this very day? Alone there, with Annie!

An exclamation from the sheriff caused him to open anguished eyes, to look up. Thomas was pointing far up the road, where a slim woman's figure could be made out, running stumblingly toward them, waving her hands.

"There she is! That's Annie now!" shouted Weston, and would have leaped from the fast-moving car had the sheriff not clamped an iron hand about his biceps.

"Think you can outrun us? Get a grip on yourself! We'll be up with her in thirty seconds!"

The brakes were applied, and with a screech and a smell of hot rubber, they came to a stop beside the panting woman. She was bareheaded, breathless; but despite the look of terror in her eyes, she was unhurt.

"Where is he? Did he get away?" demanded Thomas, the instinct of the man-hunter uppermost.

"N-no! He's locked up—" Annie had time for nothing more before Frank leaped to the roadside and crushed her in his arms, sobbing like a child.

Almost indignantly she pushed him away. "Frank! Behave yourself! This isn't a petting party, and I'm all right! Let me answer Mr.

Thomas!"

It was the big sheriff who pried her loose, lifted her into the tonneau, and almost before Weston had seated himself again, the car jumped forward.

"Now, Mrs. Weston! I begin to have hopes that you have more of a headpiece than your husband. You say Schmidt is locked up? In your house?"

She turned a troubled face to him. "Schmidt?" she repeated. "Is that his name? Well, it doesn't matter. I just knew that he wasn't a detective, and so I locked him up."

"Yes, but how? He's gone by this time, that's a safe bet. But we're right on his trail now, and I swear we'll have the twisters on him before another day."

Mrs. Weston smoothed her rumpled hair, "I don't know just what it was that made me suspicious of him! I guess it was the cat, at first. Cats are psychic; everybody knows that! They sense things that we don't. And Romeo never could endure him! Wouldn't set foot—paw I mean—into the house while he was there, I had always to put its saucer of milk outside—"

The sheriff interrupted. "Never mind the cat, Mrs. Weston. We'll see that it gets a medal, later on. Please proceed!"

"Well, he wasn't one bit like what a real detective ought to be! Oh, I never met one, of course, but I've read heaps of detective and mystery stories in magazines! And this Sanford Teller, as he called himself, didn't have one single trait like them! He didn't wear a thick, glossy black mustache, or chew a big black cigar, nor stamp around in thick-soled, square-toed boots, nor anything. And no detective would talk so freely about his clues as this man did. Of course, I didn't really suspect him at first; if I had, I should have told Frank. It was only that these things were sort of mulling in my mind. And this morning, with Frank going for such a long walk, I got to thinking of everything while I was washing the dishes; and suddenly, I saw that everything he had told us would fit the bandit just as well as it did him! Yes, even better. That gold chain; the bandit would have it, and he might show it and pretend that he found it in Mr. Hodge's writing desk, just to throw us off the track. Besides, I had been in the Hodge house, and they haven't got any old writing desk! And so it was with everything else that he called a clue; if he was the bandit, he'd have all these things on him; and as for the papers and things that seemed to prove he was a detective, why he might easily have forged them!"

Annie paused to draw breath. The car swerved to the right, and onto the road which, a mile ahead, passed the old Jarvis place. Thomas glanced at Weston. "Looks to me," he said, "as if the little woman was the thinking partner in your concern!"

Weston had the grace to blush, but made no answer save to squeeze his wife's hand.

"Well, it was just when I was beginning to work myself up into a real panic, that I heard a little noise behind me; and turning, there stood Teller—or whatever his name is—in the doorway! I thought he was sound asleep in the parlor, but there he stood, in his shirt sleeves, and with the queerest, the most awful look in his eyes as he stared at me! Oh! If I could have moved, I'd have run out of the house; but it seemed as if my legs had petrified, I just stood there and stared back. And then—I don't know how ever I managed it—I smiled at him, as naturally as I could, and said: 'Oh, Mr. Teller! My hands are all soapsuds; and would you mind just going down cellar and bringing up that ham that hangs from an iron hook? I want to parboil it for dinner!'

"Well, for a full minute—and it seemed years and years—he just stood there, staring at me; but little by little that strange light in his eyes died out, and he spoke as politely as could be. You know, Frank, he always was the politest thing? So unlike you, that it was suspicious in itself! And then he turned and went down the cellar stairs, and the minute I heard his feet on the cement floor, I rushed across the room and slammed the door and bolted it! And then I ran into his room, and took his pistol from his coat pocket, and ran and ran as fast as I could, down the road straight toward Jed Hooper's!"

She was wearing a short kitchen apron; and from its wide pocket she removed a squatty .45 gun and handed it to the sheriff.

"Mrs. Weston," he said solemnly, "my hat is off to you! If ever you need a job, you can be my deputy for life. But we certainly won't find that bird in any common ordinary cellar, when we get there!"

"Oh, but you will, Mr. Thomas! Ours isn't an ordinary cellar at all, is it, Frank? It hasn't any windows, only little slits a cat would have to squeeze to get through; and it is all stone and cement, and that kitchen door is just one tremendous oak plank, with a staple that some village blacksmith must have made before the Mexican War! He never could get out without tools or dynamite; and there were neither in the cellar. But I do hope he hasn't broken my lovely jars of pickles and peach plums and quince jelly and things. You know, Mr. Thomas, he is so destructive, that is, if he is the man you are hunting for?"

"He's the man all right," Thomas said, "And if he's still in that cellar, I'll see that the county replaces any pickles and jellies he's wrecked! Far as that goes, the neighbors will swamp you with homemade goodies soon as they hear he's a prisoner."

Their house was already in sight; it looked peaceful in the full flood of noonday sunshine, and to add to the homey appearance, Romeo sat on the doorstep, washing his face.

As the car stopped, and the four piled out almost simultaneously, Annie spoke again. "I don't hear him, and when I left he was yelling like a madman, and hammering on the door!"

Led by the sheriff, they entered the house. Not a sound greeted them save the ticking of the clock, and the friendly song of the teakettle. Peering cautiously around the door jamb, Thomas noted that the stout oak door leading down to the cellar still held. It was not even sprung. He crossed the floor; the iron staple was fast. He turned to speak to Frank, who was at his heels.

"Well, the door held! And unless he's dug himself out, he's still down there."

He leaned his head close against the sturdy plank, and called: "It's all up, Schmidt! Save yourself trouble by giving up quietly. You haven't a chance!"

There was no reply from below.

Again, louder still, Thomas called, placing his lips to the crack by the stout hinges. "I'm opening the door, Schmidt! And you're covered by three guns. The first false move, and we'll drill ye like a sieve!"

Still no answer.

The sheriff turned his head again. There was a little pallor beneath his tan, but his voice was steady, "Take your wife out of the room, Weston! Don't want any stray bullets to get her. And you might as well go, too. Your duty don't call you to horn into this; mine does."

Half reluctantly, but dragged by his wife, Weston stepped back over the line of possible fire, and into the living room. The sheriff's man crossed the kitchen and took his place by his side. Both held heavy service revolvers cocked in their right hands.

"Give me your pocket torch, Jim," Thomas said. "You throw the door wide open, and then cover it from the side."

The man nodded. There was a harsh scrape as the rusty iron staple gave, and suddenly the door stood wide flung. Down the dark stairs flamed the beam from the sheriff's flashlight.

After a moment, he spoke without turning his head.

"Nobody in sight. Well, I'm not exactly looking forward to this, but it's all a part of a sheriff's job!"

His heavy boot was planted on the topmost step. And, swinging his pocket torch in narrow arcs, illuminating every corner of the dark cellar as he advanced, his revolver held at the cock, he slowly; descended to the cement vault in which presumably, a maniac lurked ready to sell his life for the best price he could exact.

There came to those who waited above, their breaths held almost to suffocation, the pulses singing in their arteries, an astonished cry from Joe Thomas. "By thunder! Jim, come down here!"

Not only the deputy, but Frank Weston and his wife piled forward, something in the sheriff's voice telling them that there was nothing more to fear.

Nor was there. In the center of the little, snug, dry cellar, a great shelf of preserves and jellies swung gently to and fro. At one side of the cellar, something else swayed slightly, turning ever so little from side to side. Something suspended from the iron hook to which, a half hour ago, a smoked ham had been made fast.

It was their genial guest of the past four days, who, finding himself a helpless prisoner, had removed his leather belt, and hanged himself!

ASTROPHOBOS

by H.P. Lovecraft

In the Midnight heaven's burning
Through the ethereal deeps afar
Once I watch'd with restless yearning
An alluring aureate star;
Ev'ry eve aloft returning
Gleaming nigh the Arctic Car.

Mystic waves of beauty blended
With the gorgeous golden rays
Phantasies of bliss descended
In a myrrh'd Elysian haze.
In the lyre-born chords extended
Harmonies of Lydian lays.

And (thought I) lie scenes of pleasure,
Where the free and blessed dwell,
And each moment bears a treasure,
Freighted with the lotos-spell,
And there floats a liquid measure
From the lute of Israfel.

There (I told myself) were shining
Worlds of happiness unknown,

Peace and Innocence entwining
By the Crowned Virtue's throne;
Men of light, their thoughts refining
Purer, fairer, than my own.

Thus I mus'd when o'er the vision
Crept a red delirious change;
Hope dissolving to derision,
Beauty to distortion strange;
Hymnic chords in weird collision,
Spectral sights in endless range. . . .
Crimson burn'd the star of madness
As behind the beams I peer'd;
All was woe that seem'd but gladness
Ere my gaze with Truth was sear'd;
Cacodaemons, mir'd with madness,
Through the fever'd flick'ring leer'd. . . .
Now I know the fiendish fable
That the golden glitter bore;
Now I shun the spangled sable
That I watch'd and lov'd before;
But the horror, set and stable,
Haunts my soul forevermore.

SON OF THE WHITE WOLF

by Robert E. Howard

CHAPTER I
THE BATTLE STANDARD

The commander of the Turkish outpost of El Ash-rat was awakened before dawn by the stamp of horses and jingle of accoutrements. He sat up and shouted for his orderly. There was no response, so he rose, hurriedly jerked on his garments, and strode out of the mud hut that served as his headquarters. What he saw rendered him momentarily speechless.

His command was mounted, in full marching formation, drawn up near the railroad that it was their duty to guard. The plain to the left of the track where the tents of the troopers had stood now lay bare. The tents had been loaded on the baggage camels which stood fully packed and ready to move out. The commandant glared wildly, doubting his own senses, until his eyes rested on a flag borne by a trooper. The waving pennant did not display the familiar cres-

cent. The commandant turned pale.

"What does this mean?" he shouted, striding forward. His lieutenant, Osman, glanced at him inscrutably. Osman was a tall man, hard and supple as steel, with a dark keen face.

"Mutiny, *effendi,*" he replied calmly. "We are sick of this war we fight for the Germans. We are sick of Djemal Pasha and those other fools of the Council of Unity and Progress, and, incidentally, of you. So we are going to the hills to build a tribe of our own."

"Madness!" gasped the officer, tugging at his revolver. Even as he drew it, Osman shot him through the head.

The lieutenant sheathed the smoking pistol and turned to the troopers. The ranks were his to a man, won to his wild ambition under the very nose of the officer who now lay there with his brains oozing.

"Listen!" he commanded.

In the tense silence they all heard the low, deep reverberation in the west.

"British guns!" said Osman. "Battering the Turkish Empire to bits! The New Turks have failed. What Asia needs is not a new party, but a new race! There are thousands of fighting men between the Syrian coast and the Persian highlands, ready to be roused by a new word, a new prophet! The East is moving in her sleep. Ours is the duty is to awaken her!

"You have all sworn to follow me into the hills. Let us return to the ways of our pagan ancestors who worshipped the White Wolf on the steppes of High Asia before they bowed to the creed of Mohammed!

"We have reached the end of the Islamic Age. We abjure Allah as a superstition fostered by an epileptic Meccan camel driver. Our people have copied Arab ways too long. But we hundred men are *Turks!* We have burned the Koran. We bow not toward Mecca, nor swear by their false Prophet. And now follow me as we planned—to establish ourselves in a strong position in the hills and to seize Arab women for our wives."

"Our sons will be half-Arab," someone protested.

"A man is the son of his father," retorted Osman. "We Turks have always looted the *harims* of the world for our women, but our sons are always Turks.

"Come! We have arms, horses, supplies. If we linger we shall be crushed with the rest of the army between the British on the coast and the Arabs the Englishman Lawrence is bringing up from the south. On to El Awad! The sword for the men—captivity for the women!"

His voice cracked like a whip as he snapped the orders that set the lines in motion. In perfect order they moved off through the lightening dawn toward the range of saw-edged hills in the distance. Behind them the air still vibrated with the distant rumble of the British artillery. Over them waved a banner that bore the head of a white wolf—the battle-standard of most ancient Turan.

CHAPTER II
MASSACRE

When Fräulein Olga von Bruckmann, known as a famous German secret agent, arrived at the tiny Arab hill-village of El Awad, it was in a drizzling rain, that made the dusk a blinding curtain over the muddy town.

With her companion, an Arab named Ahmed, she rode into the muddy street, and the villagers crept from their hovels to stare in awe at the first white woman most of them had ever seen.

A few words from Ahmed and the *shaykh* salaamed and showed her to the best mud hut in the village. The horses were led away to feed and shelter, and Ahmed paused long enough to whisper to his companion:

"El Awad is friendly to the Turks. Have no fear. I shall be near, in any event."

"Try and get fresh horses," she urged. "I must push on as soon as possible."

"The *shaykh* swears there isn't a horse in the village in fit condition to be ridden. He may be lying. But at any rate our own horses will be rested enough to go on by dawn. Even with fresh horses it would be

useless to try to go any farther tonight. We'd lose our way among the hills, and in this region there's always the risk of running into Lawrence's Bedouin raiders."

Olga knew that Ahmed knew she carried important secret documents from Baghdad to Damascus, and she knew from experience that she could trust his loyalty. Removing only her dripping cloak and riding boots, she stretched herself on the dingy blankets that served as a bed. She was worn out from the strain of the journey.

She was the first white woman ever to attempt to ride from Baghdad to Damascus. Only the protection accorded a trusted secret agent by the long arm of the German-Turkish government, and her guide's zeal and craft, had brought her thus far in safety.

She fell asleep, thinking of the long weary miles still to be traveled, and even greater dangers, now that she had come into the region where the Arabs were fighting their Turkish masters. The Turks still held the country, that summer of 1917, but lightning-like raids flashed across the desert, blowing up trains, cutting tracks and butchering the inhabitants of isolated posts. Lawrence was leading the tribes northward, and with him was the mysterious American, *El Borak,* whose name was one to hush children.

She never knew how long she slept, but she awoke suddenly and sat up, in fright and bewilderment. The rain still beat on the roof, but there mingled with it shrieks of pain or fear, yells and the staccato crackling of rifles. She sprang up, lighted a candle and was just pulling on her boots when the door was hurled open violently.

Ahmed reeled in, his dark face livid, blood oozing through the fingers that clutched his breast.

"The village is attacked!" he cried chokingly. "Men in Turkish uniform! There must be some mistake! They know El Awad is friendly! I tried to tell their officer that we are friends, but he shot me! We must get away, quick!"

A shot cracked in the open door behind him and a jet of fire spurted from the blackness. Ahmed groaned and crumpled. Olga cried out in horror, staring wide-eyed at the figure who stood before her. A tall, wiry man in Turkish uniform blocked the door. He was handsome in a dark, hawk-like way, and he eyed her in a manner that brought the blood to her cheeks.

'Why did you kill that man?" she demanded. "He was a trusted servant of your country."

"I have no country," he answered, moving toward her. Outside the firing was dying away and women's voices were lifted piteously. "I go to build one, as my ancestor Osman did."

"I don't know what you're talking about," she retorted. "But unless you provide me with an escort to the nearest post, I shall report you to your superiors, and—"

He laughed wildly at her. "I have no superiors, you little fool! I am an empire builder, I tell you! I have a hundred armed men at my disposal. I'll build a new race in these hills." His eyes blazed as he spoke.

"You're mad!" she exclaimed.

"Mad? It's you who are mad not to recognize the possibilities as I have! This war is bleeding the life out of Europe. When it's over, no matter who wins, the nations will lie prostrate. Then it will be Asia's turn!

"If Lawrence can build up an Arab army to fight for him, then certainly I, an Ottoman, can build up a kingdom among my own peoples! Thousands of Turkish soldiers have deserted to the British. They and more will desert again to me, when they hear that a Turk is building anew the empire of ancient Turan."

"Do what you like," she answered, believing he had been seized by the madness that often grips men in time of war when the world seems crumbling and any wild dream looks possible. "But at least don't interfere with my mission. If you won't give me an escort, I'll go on alone."

"You'll go with me!" he retorted, looking down at her with hot admiration.

Olga was a handsome girl, tall, slender but supple, with a wealth of unruly golden hair. She was so completely feminine that no disguise would make her look like a man, not even the voluminous robes of an Arab, so she had attempted none. She trusted instead to Ahmed's skill to bring her safely through the desert.

"Do you hear those screams? My men are supplying themselves with wives to bear soldiers for the new empire. Yours shall be the signal honor of being the first to go into Sultan Osman's *seraglio!*"

"You do not dare!" She snatched a pistol from her blouse.

Before she could level it he wrenched it from her with brutal strength.

"Dare!" He laughed at her vain struggles. "What do I not dare? I tell you a new empire is being born tonight! Come with me! There's no time for love-making now. Before dawn we must be on the march for Sulaiman's Walls. The star of the White Wolf rises!"

CHAPTER III
THE CALL OF BLOOD

The sun was not long risen over the saw-edged mountains to the east, but already the heat was glazing the cloudless sky to the hue of white-hot steel. Along the dim road that split the immensity of the desert a single shape moved. The shape grew out of the heat-hazes of the south and resolved itself into a man on a camel.

The man was no Arab. His boots and khakis, as well as the rifle-butt jutting from beneath his knee, spoke of the West. But with his dark face and hard frame he did not look out of place, even in that fierce land. He was Francis Xavier Gordon, El Borak, whom men loved, feared or hated, according to their political complexion, from the Golden Horn to the headwaters of the Ganges.

He had ridden most of the night, but his iron frame had not yet approached the fringes of weariness. Another mile, and he sighted a yet dimmer trail straggling down from a range of hills to the east. Something was coming along this trail—a crawling something that left a broad dark smear on the hot flints.

Gordon swung his camel into the trail and a moment later bent over the man who lay there gasping stertorously. It was a young Arab, and the breast of his *abba* was soaked in blood.

"Yusef!" Gordon drew back the wet *abba*, glanced at the bared breast, then covered it again. Blood oozed steadily from a blue-rimmed bullet-hole. There was nothing he could do. Already the Arab's eyes were glazing. Gordon stared up the trail, seeing neither horse nor camel anywhere. But the dark smear stained the stones as far as he could see.

"My God, man, how far have you crawled in this condition?"

"An hour—many hours—I do not know!" panted Yusef. "I fainted and fell from the saddle. When I came to I was lying in the trail and my horse was gone. But I knew you would be coming up from the south, so I crawled—crawled! Allah, how hard are thy stones!"

Gordon set a canteen to his lips and Yusef drank noisily, then clutched Gordon's sleeve with clawing fingers.

"El Borak, I am dying and that is no great matter, but there is the matter of vengeance—not for me, *ya sidi*, but for innocent ones. You know I was on furlough to my village, El Awad. I am the only man of El Awad who fights for Arabia. The elders are friendly to the Turks. But last night the Turks burned El Awad! They marched in before midnight and the people welcomed them—while I hid in a shed.

"Then without warning they began slaying! The men of El Awad were unarmed and helpless. I slew one soldier myself. Then they shot me and I dragged myself away—found my horse and rode to tell the tale before I died. Ah, Allah, I have tasted of perdition this night!"

"Did you recognize their officer?" asked Gordon.

"I never saw him before. They called this leader of theirs Osman Pasha. Their flag bore the head of a white wolf. I saw it by the light of the burning huts. My people cried out in vain that they were friends.

"There was a German woman and a man of Hauran who came to El Awad from the east, just at nightfall. I think they were spies. The Turks shot him and took her captive. It was all blood and madness."

"Mad indeed!" muttered Gordon. Yusef lifted himself on an elbow and groped for him, a desperate urgency in his weakening voice.

"El Borak, I fought well for the Emir Feisal, and for Lawrence *effendi,* and for you! I was at Yenbo, and Wejh, and Akaba. Never have I asked a reward! I ask now: justice and vengeance! Grant me this plea: Slay the Turkish dogs who butchered my people!"

Gordon did not hesitate.

"They shall die," he answered.

Yusef smiled fiercely, gasped: *"Allaho akbar!"* then sank back dead.

Within the hour Gordon rode eastward. The vultures had already gathered in the sky with their grisly foreknowledge of death, then flapped sullenly away from the cairn of stones he had piled over the dead man, Yusef.

Gordon's business in the north could wait. One reason for his dominance over the Orientals was the fact that in some ways his nature closely resembled

theirs. He not only understood the cry for vengeance, but he sympathized with it. And he always kept his promise.

But he was puzzled. The destruction of a friendly village was not customary, even by the Turks, and certainly they would not ordinarily have mishandled their own spies. If they were deserters they were acting in an unusual manner, for most deserters made their way to Feisal. And what was that wolf's head banner?

Gordon knew that certain fanatics in the New Turks party were trying to erase all signs of Arab culture from their civilization. This was an impossible task, since that civilization itself was based on Arabic culture; but he had heard that in Istambul the radicals even advocated abandoning Islam and reverting to the paganism of their ancestors. But he had never believed the tale.

The sun was sinking over the mountains of Edom when Gordon came to ruined El Awad, in a fold of the bare hills. For hours before he had marked its location by black dots dropping in the blue sky. That they did not rise again told him that the village was deserted except for the dead.

As he rode into the dusty street, several vultures flapped heavily away. The hot sun had dried the mud, curdled the red pools in the dust. He sat in his saddle a while, staring silently.

He was no stranger to the handiwork of the Turk. He had seen much of it in the long fighting up from Jeddah on the Red Sea. But even so, he felt sick. The bodies lay in the street, headless, disemboweled, hewn asunder—bodies of children, old women and men. A red mist floated before his eyes, so that for a moment the landscape seemed to swim in blood. The slayers were gone; but they had left a plain road for him to follow.

What the signs they had left did not show him, he guessed. The slayers had loaded their female captives on baggage camels, and had gone eastward, deeper into the hills. Why they were following that road he could not guess, but he knew where it led—to the long-abandoned Walls of Sulaiman, by way of the Well of Achmet.

Without hesitation he followed. He had not gone many miles before he passed more of their work—a baby, its brains oozing from its broken head. Some kidnapped woman had hidden her child in her robes until it had been wrenched from her and brained on the rocks, before her eyes.

The country became wilder as he went. He did not halt to eat, but munched dried dates from his pouch as he rode. He did not waste time worrying over the recklessness of his action—one lone American dogging the crimson trail of a Turkish raiding party.

He had no plan; his future actions would depend on the circumstances that arose. But he had taken the death-trail and he would not turn back while he lived. He was no more foolhardy than his grandfather who single-handed trailed an Apache war party for days through the Guadalupes and returned to the settlement on the Pecos with scalps hanging from his belt.

The sun had set and dusk was closing in when Gordon topped a ridge and looked down on the plain whereon stands the Well of Achmet with its straggling palm grove. To the right of that cluster stood the tents, horse lines and camel lines of a well-ordered force. To the left stood a hut used by travelers as a *khan*. The door was shut and a sentry stood before it. While he watched, a man came from the tents with a bowl of food which he handed in at the door.

Gordon could not see the occupant, but he believed it was the German girl of whom Yusef had spoken, though why they should imprison one of their own spies was one of the mysteries of this strange affair. He saw their flag, and could make out a splotch of white that must be the wolf's head. He saw, too, the Arab women, thirty-five or forty of them herded into a pen improvised from bales and pack-saddles. They crouched together dumbly, dazed by their misfortunes.

He had hidden his camel below the ridge, on the western slope, and he lay concealed behind a clump of stunted bushes until night had fallen. Then he slipped down the slope, circling wide to avoid the mounted patrol, which rode leisurely about the camp. He lay prone behind a boulder till it had passed, then rose and stole toward the hut. Fires twinkled in the darkness beneath the palms, and he heard the wailing of the captive women.

The sentry before the door of the hut did not see the cat-footed shadow that glided up to the rear wall. As Gordon drew close he heard voices within. They spoke in Turkish.

One window was in the back wall. Strips of wood had been fastened over it, to serve as both pane and bars. Peering between them, Gordon saw a slender girl in a travel-worn riding habit standing before a dark-faced man in a Turkish uniform. There was no insignia to show what his rank had been. The Turk played with a riding whip and his eyes gleamed with cruelty in the light of a candle on a camp table.

"What do I care for the information you bring from Baghdad?" he was demanding. "Neither Turkey nor Germany means anything to me. But it seems you fail to realize your own position. It is mine to command, you to obey! You are my prisoner, my captive, my slave! It's time you learned what that means. And the best teacher I know is the whip!"

He fairly spat the last word at her and she paled.

"You dare not subject me to this indignity!" she whispered weakly.

Gordon knew this man must be Osman Pasha. He drew his heavy automatic from its scabbard under his armpit and aimed at the Turk's breast through the crack in the window. But even as his finger closed on the trigger he changed his mind. There was the sentry at the door, and a hundred other armed men, within hearing, whom the sound of a shot would bring on the run. He grasped the window bars and braced his legs.

"I see I must dispel your illusions," muttered Osman, moving toward the girl who cowered back until the wall stopped her. Her face was white. She had dealt with many dangerous men in her hazardous career, and she was not easily frightened. But she had never met a man like Osman. His face was a terrifying mask of cruelty; the ferocity that gloats over the agony of a weaker thing shone in his eyes.

Suddenly he had her by the hair, dragging her to him, laughing at her scream of pain. Just then Gordon ripped the strips off the window. The snapping of the wood sounded loud as a gunshot and Osman wheeled, drawing his pistol, as Gordon came through the window.

The American lit on his feet, and leveled his auto-

matic, checking Osman's move. The Turk froze, his pistol lifted shoulder high, muzzle pointing at the roof. Outside the sentry called anxiously.

"Answer him!" grated Gordon below his breath. "Tell him everything is all right. And drop that gun!"

The pistol fell to the floor and the girl snatched it up.

"Come here, *Fräulein*!"

She ran to him, but in her haste she crossed the line of fire. In that fleeting moment when her body shielded his, Osman acted. He kicked the table and the candle toppled and went out, and simultaneously he dived for the floor. Gordon's pistol roared deafeningly just as the hut was plunged into darkness. The next instant the door crashed inward and the sentry bulked against the starlight, to crumple as Gordon's gun crashed again and yet again.

With a sweep of his arm, Gordon found the girl and drew her toward the window. He lifted her through as if she had been a child, and climbed through after her. He did not know whether his blind slug had struck Osman or not. The man was crouching silently in the darkness, but there was no time to strike a match and see whether he was living or dead. But as they ran across the shadowy plain, they heard Osman's voice lifted in passion.

By the time they reached the crest of the ridge, the girl was winded. Only Gordon's arm about her waist, half-dragging, half-carrying her, enabled her to make the last few yards of the steep incline. The plain below them was alive with torches and shouting men. Osman was yelling for them to run down the fugitive, and his voice came faintly to them on the ridge.

"Take them alive, curse you! Scatter and find them! It's El Borak!" An instant later he was yelling, with an edge of panic in his voice: "Wait. Come back! Take cover and make ready to repel an attack! He may have a horde of Arabs with him!"

"He thinks first of his own desire, and only later of the safety of his men," muttered Gordon. "I don't think he'll ever get very far. Come on."

He led the way to the camel, helped the girl into the saddle, then leaped up himself. A word, a tap of the camel wand, and the beast ambled silently off down the slope.

"I know Osman caught you at El Awad," said Gordon. "But what's he up to? What's his game?"

"He was a lieutenant stationed at El Ashraf," she answered. "He persuaded his company to mutiny, kill their commander, and desert. He plans to fortify the Walls of Sulaiman, and build a new empire. I thought at first he was mad, but he isn't. He's a devil."

"The Walls of Sulaiman?" Gordon checked his mount and sat for a moment motionless in the starlight.

"Are you game for an all-night ride?" he asked presently.

"Anywhere! As long as it is far away from Osman!" There was a hint of hysteria in her voice.

"I doubt if your escape will change his plans. He'll probably lie about Achmet all night under arms expecting an attack. In the morning he will decide that I was alone, and pull out for the Walls.

"Well, I happen to know that an Arab force is there, waiting for an order from Lawrence to move on to Ageyli. Three hundred Juheina camel-riders, sworn to Feisal. Enough to eat Osman's gang. Lawrence's messenger should reach them some time between dawn and noon. There is a chance we can get there before the Juheina pull out. If we can, we'll turn them on Osman and wipe him out, with his whole pack.

"It won't upset Lawrence's plans for the Juheina to get to Ageyli a day late, and Osman must be destroyed. He's a mad dog running loose."

"His ambition sounds mad," she murmured. "But when he speaks of it, with his eyes blazing, it's easy to believe he might even succeed."

"You forget that crazier things have happened in the desert," he answered, as he swung the camel eastward. "The world is being made over here, as well as in Europe. There's no telling what damage this

Osman might do, if left to himself. The Turkish Empire is falling to pieces, and new empires *have* risen out of the ruins of old ones.

"But if we can get to Sulaiman before the Juheina march, we'll check him. If we find them gone, we'll be in a pickle ourselves. It's a gamble, our lives against his. Are you game?"

"Till the last card falls!" she retorted. His face was a blur in the starlight, but she sensed rather than saw his grim smile of approval.

The camel's hoofs made no sound as they dropped down the slope and circled far wide of the Turkish camp. Like ghosts on a ghost-camel they moved across the plain under the stars. A faint breeze stirred the girl's hair. Not until the fires were dim behind them and they were again climbing a hill-road, did she speak.

"I know you. You're the American they call El Borak, the Swift. You came down from Afghanistan when the war began. You were with King Hussein even before Lawrence came over from Egypt. Do you know who I am?"

"Yes."

"Then what's my status?" she asked. "Have you rescued me or captured me? Am I a prisoner?"

"Let us say companion, for the time being," he suggested. "We're up against a common enemy. No reason why we shouldn't make common cause, is there?"

"None!" she agreed, and leaning her blond head against his hard shoulder, she went soundly to sleep.

A gaunt moon rose, pushing back the horizons, flooding craggy slopes and dusty plains with leprous silver. The vastness of the desert seemed to mock the tiny figures on their tiring camel, as they rode blindly on toward what Fate they could not guess.

CHAPTER IV
WOLVES OF THE DESERT

Olga awoke as dawn was breaking. She was cold and stiff, in spite of the cloak Gordon had wrapped about her, and she was hungry. They were riding through a dry gorge with rock-strewn slopes rising on either hand, and the camel's gait had become a lurching walk. Gordon halted it, slid off without making it kneel, and took its rope.

"It's about done, but the Walls aren't far ahead. Plenty of water there—food, too, if the Juheina are still there. There are dates in that pouch."

If he felt the strain of fatigue he did not show it as he strode along at the camel's head. Olga rubbed her chill hands and wished for sunrise.

"The Well of Harith," Gordon indicated a walled enclosure ahead of them. "The Turks built that wall, years ago, when the Walls of Sulaiman were an army post. Later they abandoned both positions."

The wall, built of rocks and dried mud, was in good shape; and inside the enclosure there was a partly ruined hut. The well was shallow, with a mere trickle of water at the bottom.

"I'd better get off and walk too," Olga suggested.

"These flints would cut your boots and feet to pieces. It's not far now. Then the camel can rest all it needs."

"And if the Juheina aren't there—" She left the sentence unfinished.

He shrugged his shoulders.

"Maybe Osman won't come up before the camel's rested."

"I believe he'll make a forced march," she said, not fearfully, but calmly stating an opinion. "His beasts are good. If he drives them hard, he can get here before midnight. Our camel won't be rested enough to carry us by that time. And we couldn't get away on foot, in this desert."

He laughed, and respecting her courage, did not try to make light of their position.

"Well," he said quietly, "let's hope the Juheina are still there!"

If they were not, she and Gordon were caught in a trap of hostile, waterless desert, fanged with the long guns of predatory tribesmen.

Three miles further east the valley narrowed and the floor pitched upward, dotted by dry shrubs and boulders. Gordon pointed suddenly to a faint ribbon of smoke feathering up into the sky.

"Look! The Juheina are there!"

Olga gave a deep sigh of relief. Only then, did she realize how desperately she had been hoping for some such sign. She felt like shaking a triumphant fist at the rocky waste about her, as if at a sentient enemy, sullen and cheated of its prey.

Another mile and they topped a ridge and saw a large enclosure surrounding a cluster of wells. There were Arabs squatting about their tiny cooking fires. As the travelers came suddenly into view within a few hundred yards of them, the Bedouins sprang up, shouting. Gordon drew his breath suddenly between clenched teeth.

"They are not Juheina! They're Rualla! Allies of the Turks!"

Too late to retreat. A hundred and fifty wild men were on their feet, glaring, rifles cocked.

Gordon did the next best thing and went leisurely toward them. To look at him one would have thought that he had expected to meet these men here, and anticipated nothing but a friendly greeting. Olga tried to imitate his tranquility, but she knew their lives hung on the crook of a trigger finger. These men were supposed to be her allies, but her recent experience made her distrust Orientals. The sight of these hundreds of wolfish faces filled her with sick dread.

They were hesitating, rifles lifted, nervous and uncertain as surprised wolves, then:

"Allah!" howled a tall, scarred warrior. "It is El Borak!"

Olga caught her breath as she saw the man's finger quiver on his rifle-trigger. Only a racial urge to gloat over his victim kept him from shooting the American, then and there.

"El Borak!" The shout was a wave that swept the throng.

Ignoring the clamor, the menacing rifles, Gordon made the camel kneel and lifted Olga off. She tried, with fair success, to conceal her fear of the wild figures that crowded about them, but her flesh crawled at the blood-lust burning redly in each wolfish eye.

Gordon's rifle was in its boot on the saddle, and his pistol was out of sight, under his shirt. He was careful not to reach for the rifle – a move which would have brought a hail of bullets—but having helped the girl down, he turned and faced the crowd casually, his hands empty. Running his glance over the fierce faces, he singled out a tall stately man in the rich garb of a *shaykh*, who was standing somewhat apart.

"You keep poor watch, Mitkhal ibn Ali," said Gordon. "If I had been a raider your men would be lying in their blood by this time."

Before the *shaykh* could answer, the man who had first recognized Gordon thrust himself violently forward, his face convulsed with hate.

"You expected to find friends here, El Borak!" he exulted. "But you come too late! Three hundred Juheina dogs rode north an hour before dawn! We saw them go, and came up after they had gone. Had they known of your coming, perhaps they would have stayed to welcome you!"

"It's not to you I speak, Zangi Khan, you Kurdish dog," retorted Gordon contemptuously, "but to the Rualla—honorable men and fair foes!"

Zangi Khan snarled like a wolf and threw up his rifle, but a lean Bedouin caught his arm.

"Wait!" he growled. "Let El Borak speak. His words are not wind."

A rumble of approval came from the Arabs. Gordon had touched their fierce pride and vanity. That would not save his life, but they were willing to listen to him before they killed him.

"If you listen, he will trick you with cunning words!" shouted the angered Zangi Khan furiously. "Slay him now, before he can do us harm!"

"Is Zangi Khan *shaykh* of the Rualla that he gives his commands while Mitkhal stands silent?" asked Gordon with biting irony.

Mitkhal reacted to his taunt exactly as Gordon knew he would.

"Let El Borak speak!" he ordered. "I command here, Zangi Khan! Do not forget that."

"I do not forget, *ya sidi*," the Kurd assured him, but his eyes burned red at the rebuke. "I but spoke in zeal for your safety."

Mitkhal gave him a slow, searching glance which told Gordon that there was no love lost between the two men. Zangi Khan's reputation as a fighting man meant much to the younger warriors. Mitkhal was more fox than wolf, and he evidently feared the Kurd's influence over his men. As an agent of the Turkish government Zangi's authority was theoretically equal to Mitkhal's. Actually this amounted to little, for Mitkhal's tribesmen took orders from their *shaykh* only. But it put Zangi in a position to use his personal talents to gain an ascendancy—an ascendancy Mitkhal feared would relegate him to a minor position.

"Speak, El Borak," ordered Mitkhal. "But speak swiftly. It may be," he added, "Allah's will that the moments of your life are few."

"Death marches from the west," said Gordon abruptly. "Last night a hundred Turkish deserters butchered the people of El Awad."

"Wallah!" swore a tribesman. "El Awad was friendly to the Turks!"

"A lie!" cried Zangi Khan. "Or if true, the dogs of deserters slew the people to curry favor with Feisal."

"When did men come to Feisal with the blood of children on their hands?" retorted Gordon. "They have foresworn Islam and worship the White Wolf. They carried off the young women and the old women, the men and the children they slew like dogs."

A murmur of anger rose from the Arabs. The Bedouins had a rigid code of warfare, and they did not kill women or children. It was the unwritten law of the desert, old when Abraham came up out of Chaldea.

But Zangi Khan cried out in angry derision, blind to the resentful looks cast at him. He did not understand that particular phase of the Bedouins' code, for his people had no such inhibition. Kurds in war killed women as well as men.

"What are the women of El Awad to us?" he sneered.

"Your heart I know already," answered Gordon with icy contempt. "It is to the Rualla that I speak."

"A trick!" howled the Kurd. "A lie to trick us!"

"It is no lie!" Olga stepped forward boldly. "Zangi Khan, you know that I am an agent of the German government. Osman Pasha, leader of these renegades, burned El Awad last night, as El Borak has said. Osman murdered Ahmed ibn Shalaan, my guide, among others. He is as much our enemy as he is an enemy of the British."

She looked to Mitkhal for help, but the *shaykh* stood apart, like an actor watching a play in which he had not yet received his cue.

"What if it is the truth?" Zangi Khan snarled, muddled by his hate and fear of El Borak's cunning. "What is El Awad to us?"

Gordon caught him up instantly.

"This Kurd asks what is the destruction of a friendly village! Doubtless, naught to him! But what does it mean to you, who have left your herds and families unguarded? If you let this pack of mad dogs range the land, how can you be sure of the safety of your wives and children?"

"What would you have, El Borak?" demanded a gray-bearded raider.

"Trap these Turks and destroy them. I'll show you how."

It was then that Zangi Khan lost his head completely.

"Heed him not!" he screamed. "Within the hour we must ride northward! The Turks will give us ten thousand British pounds for his head!"

Avarice burned briefly in the men's eyes, to be dimmed by the reflection that the reward, offered for El Borak's head, would be claimed by the *shaykh* and Zangi. They made no move and Mitkhal stood aside with an air of watching a contest that did not concern himself.

"Take his head!" screamed Zangi, sensing hostility at last, and thrown into a panic by it.

His demoralization was completed by Gordon's taunting laugh.

"You seem to be the only one who wants my head, Zangi! Perhaps you can take it!"

Zangi howled incoherently, his eyes glaring red, then threw up his rifle, hip-high. Just as the muzzle came up, Gordon's automatic crashed thunderously. He had drawn so swiftly not a man there had followed his motion. Zangi Khan reeled back under the impact of hot lead, toppled sideways and lay still.

In an instant, a hundred cocked rifles covered Gordon. Confused by varying emotions, the men hesitated for the fleeting instant it took Mitkhal to shout:

"Hold! Do not shoot!"

He strode forward with the air of a man ready to take the center of the stage at last, but he could not disguise the gleam of satisfaction in his shrewd eyes.

"No man here is kin to Zangi Khan," he said offhandedly. There is no cause for blood feud. He had eaten the salt, but he attacked our prisoner, whom he thought unarmed."

He held out his hand for the pistol, but Gordon did not surrender it.

"I'm not your prisoner," said he. "I could kill you before your men could lift a finger. But I didn't come here to fight you. I came asking aid to avenge the children and women of my enemies. I risk my life for your families. Are you dogs, to do less?"

The question hung in the air unanswered, but he had struck the right chord in their barbaric bosoms, that were always ready to respond to some wild deed of reckless chivalry. Their eyes glowed and they looked at their *shaykh* expectantly.

Mitkhal was a shrewd politician. The butchery at El Awad meant much less to him than it meant to his younger warriors. He had associated with so-called civilized men long enough to lose much of his primitive integrity. But he always followed the side of public opinion, and was shrewd enough to lead a movement he could not check. Yet, he was not to be stampeded into a hazardous adventure.

"These Turks may be too strong for us," he objected.

"I'll show you how to destroy them with little risk," answered Gordon. "But there must be covenants between us, Mitkhal."

"These Turks must be destroyed," said Mitkhal, and he spoke sincerely there, at least. "But there are too many blood feuds between us, El Borak, for us to let you get out of our hands."

Gordon laughed.

"You can't whip the Turks without my help, and you know it. Ask your young men what they desire!"

"Let El Borak lead us!" shouted a young warrior instantly. A murmur of approval paid tribute to Gordon's widespread reputation as a strategist.

"Very well!" Mitkhal took the tide. "Let there be truce between us—with conditions! Lead us against the Turks. If you win, you and the woman shall go free. If we lose, we take your head!"

Gordon nodded, and the warriors yelled in glee. It was just the sort of a bargain that appealed to their minds, and Gordon knew it was the best he could make.

"Bring bread and salt!" ordered Mitkhal, and a giant black slave moved to do his bidding. "Until the battle is lost or won there is truce between us, and no Rualla shall harm you, unless you spill Rualla blood."

Then he thought of something else and his brow darkened as he thundered:

"Where is the man who watched from the ridge?"

A terrified youth was pushed forward. He was a member of a small tribe tributary to the more important Rualla.

"Oh, *shaykh*," he faltered, "I was hungry and stole away to a fire for meat—"

"Dog!" Mitkhal struck him in the face. "Death is thy portion for failing in thy duty."

"Wait!" Gordon interposed. "Would you question the will of Allah? If the boy had not deserted his post he would have seen us coming up the valley, and your men would have fired on us and killed us. Then you would not have been warned of the Turks, and would have fallen prey to them before discovering they were enemies. Let him go and give thanks to Allah, Who sees all!"

It was the sort of sophistry that appeals to the Arab mind. Even Mitkhal was impressed.

"Who knows the mind of Allah?" he conceded. "Live, Musa, but next time perform the will of Allah with a vigilance and a mind to orders. And now, El Borak, let us discuss battle-plans while food is prepared."

CHAPTER V
TREACHERY

It was not yet noon when Gordon halted the Rualla beside the Well of Harith. Scouts sent westward reported no sign of the Turks, and the Arabs went forward with the plans made before leaving the Walls—plans outlined by Gordon and agreed to by Mitkhal. First the tribesmen began gathering rocks and hurling them into the well.

"The water's still beneath," Gordon remarked to Olga, "but it'll take hours of hard work to clean out the well so that anybody can get to it. The Turks can't do it under our rifles. If we win, we'll clean it out ourselves, so the next travelers won't suffer."

"Why not take refuge in the *sangar* ourselves?" she asked.

"Too much of a trap. That's what we're using it for. We'd have no chance with them in open fight, and if we laid an ambush out in the valley, they'd simply fight their way through us. But when a man's shot at in the open, his first instinct is to make for the nearest cover. So I'm hoping to trick them into going into the *sangar*. Then we'll bottle them up and pick them off at our leisure. Without water they can't hold out long. We shouldn't lose a dozen men, if any."

"It seems strange to see you solicitous about the lives of these Rualla, who are your enemies, after all," she laughed.

"Instinct, maybe. No man fit to lead wants to lose any more of them then he can help. Just now these men are my allies, and it's up to me to protect them as well as I can. I'll admit I'd rather be fighting with the Juheina. Feisal's messenger must have started for the Walls hours before I supposed he would."

"And if the Turks surrender, what then?"

"I'll try to get them to Lawrence—all but Osman Pasha." Gordon's face darkened. "That man hangs if he falls into my hands."

"How will you get them to Lawrence? The Rualla won't take them."

"I haven't the slightest idea. But let's catch our hare before we start broiling him. Osman may whip the daylights out of us."

"It means your head if he does," she warned, with a shudder.

"Well, it's worth ten thousand pounds to the Turks," he laughed, and moved to inspect the partly ruined hut. Olga followed him.

Mitkhal, directing the blocking of the well, glanced sharply at them, then noted that a number of men were between them and the gate, and turned back to his overseeing.

"*Hsss*, El Borak!" It was a tense whisper, just as Gordon and Olga turned to leave the hut. An instant later they located a tousled head thrust up from behind a heap of rubble. It was the boy Musa, who obviously had slipped into the hut through a crevice in the back wall.

"Watch from the door and warn me if you see anybody coming," Gordon muttered to Olga. "This lad may have something to tell."

"I have, *effendi*!" The boy was trembling with excitement. "I overheard the *shaykh* talking secretly to his black slave, Hassan. I saw them walk away among the palms while you and the woman were eating, at the Walls, and I crept after them, for I feared they meant you mischief—and you saved my life."

"El Borak, listen! Mitkal means to slay you, whether you win this battle for him or not! He was glad you slew the Kurd, and he is glad to have your aid in wiping out these Turks. But he lusts for the gold the other Turks will pay for your head. Yet he dares not break his word and the covenant of the salt openly. So, if we win the battle, Hassan is to shoot you, and swear you fell by a Turkish bullet!"

The boy rushed on with his story:

"Then Mitkhal will say to the people: 'El Borak was our guest and ate our salt. But now he is dead, through no fault of ours, and there is no use wasting the reward. So, we will take off his head and take it to Damascus, and the Turks will give us ten thousand pounds.'"

Gordon smiled grimly at Olga's horror. That was typical Arab logic.

"It didn't occur to Mitkhal that Hassan might miss his first shot and not get a chance to shoot again, I suppose?" he suggested.

"Oh, yes, *effendi*, Mitkhal thinks of everything. If you kill Hassan, Mitkhal will swear you broke the covenant yourself, by spilling the blood of a Rualla, or a Rualla's servant, which is the same thing, and will feel free to order you beheaded."

There was genuine humor in Gordon's laugh.

"Thanks, Musa! If I saved your life, you've paid me back. Better get out now, before somebody sees you talking to us."

"What shall we do?" exclaimed Olga, pale to the lips.

"You're in no danger," he assured her.

She colored angrily.

"I wasn't thinking of that! Do you think I have less gratitude than that Arab boy? That *shaykh* means to murder you, don't you understand? Let's steal camels, and run for it!"

"Run where? If we did, they'd be on our heels in no time, deciding I'd lied to them about everything. Anyway, we wouldn't have a chance. They're watching us too closely. Besides, I wouldn't run if could. I started to wipe out Osman Pasha, and this is the best chance I see to do it. Come on. Let's get out in the *sangar* before Mitkhal gets suspicious."

As soon as the well was blocked the men retired to the hillsides. Their camels were hidden behind the ridges, and the men crouched behind rocks and among the stunted shrubs along the slopes. Olga refused Gordon's offer to send her with an escort back to the Walls, and stayed with him taking up a position behind a rock, Osman's pistol in her belt. They lay flat on the ground and the heat of the sun-baked flints seeped through their garments.

Once she turned her head, and shuddered to see the blank black countenance of Hassan regarding them from some bushes a few yards behind them. The black slave, who knew no law but his master's command, was determined not to let Gordon out of his sight.

She spoke of this in a low whisper to the American.

"Sure," he murmured. "I saw him. But he won't shoot till he knows which way the fight's going, and is sure none of the men are looking."

Olga's flesh crawled in anticipation of more horrors. If they lost the fight the enraged Ruallas would tear Gordon to pieces, supposing he survived the encounter. If they won, his reward would be a treacherous bullet in the back.

The hours dragged slowly by. Not a flutter of cloth, no lifting of an impatient head betrayed the presence of the wild men on the slopes. Olga began to feel her nerves quiver. Doubts and forebodings gnawed maddeningly at her.

"We took position too soon! The men will lose patience. Osman can't get here before midnight. It took us all night to reach the Well."

"Bedouins never lose patience when they smell loot," he answered. "I believe Osman will get here before sundown. We made poor time on a tiring camel for the last few hours of that ride. I believe Osman broke camp before dawn and pushed hard."

Another thought came to torture her.

"Suppose he doesn't come at all? Suppose he has changed his plans and gone somewhere else? The Rualla will believe you lied to them!"

"Look!"

The sun hung low in the west, a fiery, dazzling ball. She blinked, shading her eyes.

Then the head of a marching column grew out of the dancing heat waves: lines of horsemen, grey with dust, files of heavily laden baggage camels, with the captive women riding them. The standard hung loose in the breathless air; but once, when a vagrant gust of wind, hot as the breath of perdition, lifted the folds, the white wolf's head was displayed.

Crushing proof of idolatry and heresy! In their agitation, the Rualla almost betrayed themselves. Even Mitkhal turned pale.

"Allah! Sacrilege! Forgotten of God. Hell shall be thy portion!"

"Easy!" hissed Gordon, feeling the semi-hysteria that ran down the lurking lines. "Wait for my signal. They may halt to water their camels at the Well."

Osman must have driven his people like a fiend all day. The women drooped on the loaded camels; the dust-caked faces of the soldiers were drawn. The horses reeled with weariness. But it was soon evident that they did not intend halting at the Well with their goal, the Walls of Sulaiman, so near. The head of the column was even with the *sangar* when Gordon fired. He was aiming at Osman, but the range was long, the sun glare on the rocks dazzling. The man behind Osman fell, and at the signal the slopes came alive with spurting flame.

The column staggered. Horses and men went down and stunned soldiers gave back a ragged fire that did no harm. They did not even see their assailants save as bits of white cloth bobbing among the boulders.

Perhaps discipline had grown lax during the grind of that merciless march. Perhaps panic seized the tired Turks. At any rate, the column broke and men fled toward the *sangar* without waiting for orders. They would have abandoned the baggage camels had not Osman ridden among them. Cursing and striking with the flat of his saber, he made them drive the beasts in with them.

"I hoped they'd leave the camels and women outside," grunted Gordon. "Maybe they'll drive them out when they find there's no water."

The Turks took their positions in good order, dismounting and ranging along the wall. Some dragged the Arab women off the camels and drove them into the hut. Others improvised a pen for the animals with stakes and ropes between the back of the hut and the wall. Saddles were piled in the gate to complete the barricade.

The Arabs yelled taunts as they poured in a hail of lead, and a few leaped up and danced derisively, waving their rifles. But they stopped that when a Turk drilled one of them cleanly through the head. When the demonstrations ceased, the besiegers offered scanty targets to shoot at.

However, the Turks fired back frugally and with no indication of panic, now that they were under cover and fighting the sort of a fight they understood. They were well protected by the wall from the men directly in front of them, but those facing north could be seen by the men on the south ridge, and vice versa. But the distance was too great for consistently effective shooting at these marks by the Arabs.

"We don't seem to be doing much damage," remarked Olga presently.

"Thirst will win for us," Gordon answered. "All we've got to do is to keep them bottled up. They probably have enough water in their canteens to last through the rest of the day. Certainly no longer. Look, they're going to the well now."

The well stood in the middle of the enclosure, in a comparatively exposed area, as seen from above. Olga saw men approaching it with canteens in their hands, and the Arabs, with sardonic enjoyment, refrained from firing at them. They reached the well, and then the girl saw the change that came over them. It ran through their band like an electric shock. The men along the walls reacted by firing wildly. A furious yelling rose, edged with hysteria, and men began to run madly about the enclosure. Some toppled, hit by shots dropping from the ridges.

"What are they doing?" Olga started to her knees, and was instantly jerked down again by Gordon. The Turks were running into the hut. If she had been watching Gordon she would have sensed the meaning of it, for his dark face grew suddenly grim.

"They're dragging the women out!" she exclaimed. "I see Osman waving his saber. What? Oh, God! They're butchering the women!"

Above the crackle of shots rose terrible shrieks and the sickening *chack* of savagely driven blows. Olga turned sick and hid her face. Osman had realized the trap into which he had been driven, and his reaction was that of a mad dog. Recognizing defeat in the blocked well, facing the ruin of his crazy ambitions by thirst and Bedouin bullets, he was taking this vengeance on the whole Arab race.

On all sides the Arabs rose howling, driven to frenzy by the sight of that slaughter. That these women were of another tribe made no difference. A stern chivalry was the foundation of their society, just as it was among the frontiersmen of early America. There was no sentimentalism about it. It was real and vital as life itself.

The Rualla went berserk when they saw women of their race falling under the swords of the Turks. A wild yell shattered the brazen sky, and recklessly breaking cover, the Arabs pelted down the slopes, howling like fiends. Gordon could not check them, nor could Mitkhal. Their shouts fell on deaf ears. The walls vomited smoke and flame as withering volleys raked the oncoming hordes. Dozens fell, but enough were left to reach the wall and sweep over it in a wave that neither lead nor steel could halt.

And Gordon was among them. When he saw he could not stop the storm he joined it. Mitkhal was not far behind him, cursing his men as he ran. The *shaykh* had no stomach for this kind of fighting, but his leadership was at stake. No man who hung back in this charge would ever be able to command the Rualla again.

Gordon was among the first to reach the wall, leaping over the writhing bodies of half a dozen Arabs. He had not blazed away wildly as he ran like the Bedouins, to reach the wall with an empty gun. He held his fire until the flame spurts from the barrier were almost burning his face, and then emptied his rifle in a point-blank fusillade that left a bloody gap where there had been a line of fierce dark faces an instant before. Before the gap could be closed he had swarmed over and in, and the Rualla poured after him.

As his feet hit the ground a rush of men knocked him against the wall and a blade, thrusting for his life, broke against the rocks. He drove his shortened butt into a snarling face, splintering teeth and bones, and the next instant a surge of his own men over the wall cleared a space about him. He threw away his broken rifle and drew his pistol.

The Turks had been forced back from the wall in a dozen places now, and men were fighting all over the *sangar*. No quarter was asked—none given. The pitiful headless bodies sprawled before the bloodstained hut had turned the Bedouins into hot-eyed demons. The guns were empty now, all but Gordon's automatic. The yells had died down to grunts, punctuated by death-howls. Above these sounds rose the chopping impact of flailing blades, the crunch of fiercely driven rifle butts. So grimly had the Bedouins suffered in that brainless rush, that now they were outnumbered, and the Turks fought with the fury of desperation.

It was Gordon's automatic, perhaps, that tipped the balance. He emptied it without haste and without hesitation, and at that range he could not miss. He was aware of a dark shadow forever behind him, and turned once to see black Hassan following him, smiting methodically right and left with a heavy scimitar already dripping crimson. Even in the fury of strife, Gordon grinned. The literal-minded Soudanese was obeying his instructions to keep at El Borak's heels. As long as the battle hung in doubt, he was Gordon's protector—ready to become his executioner the instant the tide turned in their favor.

"Faithful servant," called Gordon sardonically. "Have care lest these Turks cheat you of my head!"

Hassan grinned, speechless. Suddenly blood burst from his thick lips and he buckled at the knees. Somewhere in that rush down the hill his black body had stopped a bullet. As he struggled on all fours a Turk ran in from the side and brained him with a rifle-butt. Gordon killed the Turk with his last bullet. He felt no grudge against Hassan. The man had been a good soldier, and had obeyed orders given him.

The *sangar* was a shambles. The men on their feet were less than those on the ground, and all were streaming blood. The white wolf standard had been torn from its staff and lay trampled under vengeful feet. Gordon bent, picked up a saber and looked about for Osman. He saw Mitkhal, running toward the horse-pen, and then he yelled a warning, for he saw Osman.

The man broke away from a group of struggling figures and ran for the pen. He tore away the ropes and the horses, frantic from the noise and smell of blood, stampeded into the *sangar,* knocking men down and trampling them. As they thundered past, Osman, with a magnificent display of agility, caught a handful of flying mane and leaped on the back of the racing steed.

Mitkhal ran toward him, yelling furiously, and snapping a pistol at him. The *shaykh,* in the confusion of the fighting, did not seem to be aware that the gun was empty, for he pulled the trigger again and again as he stood in the path of the oncoming rider. Only at the last moment did he realize his peril and leap back. Even so, he would have sprung clear had not his sandal heel caught in a dead man's *abba.*

Mitkhal stumbled, avoided the lashing hoofs, but not the downflailing saber in Osman's hand. A wild cry went up from the Rualla as Mitkhal fell, his turban suddenly crimson. The next instant Osman was out of the gate and riding like the wind—straight up the hillside to where he saw the slim figure of the

girl to whom he now attributed his overthrow.

Olga had come out from behind the rocks and was standing in stunned horror watching the fight below. Now she awoke suddenly to her own peril at the sight of the madman charging up the slope. She drew the pistol Gordon had taken from him and opened fire. She was not a very good shot. Three bullets missed, the fourth killed the horse, and then the gun jammed. Gordon was running up the slope as the Apaches of his native Southwest run, and behind him streamed a swarm of Rualla. There was not a loaded gun in the whole horde.

Osman took a shocking fall when his horse turned a somersault under him, but rose, bruised and bloody, with Gordon still some distance away. But the Turk had to play hide-and-seek for a few moments among the rocks with his prey before he was able to grasp her hair and twist her screaming to her knees, and then he paused an instant to enjoy her despair and terror. That pause was his undoing.

As he lifted his saber to strike off her head, steel clanged loud on steel. A numbing shock ran through his arm, and his blade was knocked from his hand. His weapon rang on the hot flints. He whirled to face the blazing slits that were El Borak's eyes. The muscles stood out in cords and ridges on Gordon's sun burnt forearm in the intensity of his passion.

"Pick it up, you filthy dog," he said between his teeth.

Osman hesitated, stooped, caught up the saber and slashed at Gordon's legs without straightening. Gordon leaped back, then sprang in again the instant his toes touched the earth. His return was as paralyzingly quick as the death-leap of a wolf. It caught Osman off balance, his sword extended. Gordon's blade hissed as it cut the air, slicing through flesh, gritting through bone.

The Turk's head toppled from the severed neck and fell at Gordon's feet, the headless body collapsing in a heap. With an excess spasm of hate, Gordon kicked the head savagely down the slope.

"Oh!" Olga turned away and hid her face. But the girl knew that Osman deserved any fate that could have overtaken him. Presently she was aware of Gordon's hand resting lightly on her shoulder and she looked up, ashamed of her weakness. The sun was just dipping below the western ridges. Musa came limping up the slope, bloodstained but radiant.

"The dogs are all dead, *effendi!*"

he cried, industriously shaking a plundered watch, in an effort to make it run. "Such of our warriors as still live are faint from strife, and many sorely wounded. There is none to command now but thou."

"Sometimes problems settle themselves," mused Gordon. "But at a ghastly price. If the Rualla hadn't made that rush, which was the death of Hassan and Mitkhal—oh, well, such things are in the hands of Allah, as the Arabs say. A hundred better men than I have died today, but by the decree of some blind Fate, I live."

Gordon looked down on the wounded men. He turned to Musa.

"We must load the wounded on camels," he said, "and take them to the camp at the Walls where there's water and shade. Come."

As they started down the slope, he said to Olga:

"I'll have to stay with them till they're settled at the Walls, then I must start for the coast. Some of the Rualla will be able to ride, though, and you need have no fear of them. They'll escort you to the near-est Turkish outpost."

She looked at him in surprise.

"Then I'm not your prisoner?"

He laughed.

"I think you can help Feisal more by carrying out your original instructions of supplying misleading information to the Turks! I don't blame you for not confiding even in me. You have my deepest admira-tion, for you're playing the most dangerous game a woman can."

"Oh!" She felt a sudden warm flood of relief and gladness that he should know she was not really an enemy. Musa was well out of earshot. "I might have known you were high enough in Feisal's councils to know that I really am—"

"Gloria Willoughby, the cleverest, most daring secret agent the British government employs," he murmured. The girl impulsively placed her slender fingers in his, and hand in hand they went down the slope together.

ALWAYS COMES EVENING

by Robert E. Howard

Riding down the road at evening with the stars for steed and shoon
I have heard an old man singing underneath a copper moon;
"God, who gemmed with topaz twilights, opal portals of the day,
"On your amaranthine mountains, why make human souls of clay?

"For I rode the moon-mare's horses in the glory of my youth,
"Wrestled with the hills at sunset—till I met brass-tinctured Truth.
"Till I saw the temples topple, till I saw the idols reel,
"Till my brain had turned to iron, and my heart had turned to steel.

"Satan, Satan, brother Satan, fill my soul with frozen fire;
"Feed with hearts of rose-white women ashes of my dead desire.
"For my road runs out in thistles and my dreams have turned to dust.
"And my pinions fade and falter to the raven-wings of rust.

"Truth has smitten me with arrows and her hand is in my hair—
"Youth, she hides in yonder mountains—go and seek her, if you dare!
"Work your magic, brother Satan, fill my brain with fiery spells.
"Satan, Satan, brother Satan, I have known your fiercest Hells."

Riding down the road at evening when the wind was on the sea,
I have heard an old man singing, and he sang most drearily.
Strange to hear, when dark lakes shimmer to the wailing of the loon,
Amethystine Homer singing under evening's copper moon.

THE MORGUE
by Our Readers

Dan Nelson writes:

Just finished the book edition [of #3] and I was impressed with the range of the writing. I was kind of expecting some fast paced stories but I found a good variety of tales, "Forbidden Fruit" and "Moon-Calves" especially. "Pirates' Gold" was more in line with what I expected and was a real good read. Thanks. ("Floating Island," by Philip M. Fisher, was pretty cool too.)

Thanks, Dan. We try to include a wide variety of stories in every issue of ADVENTURE TALES. Let us know what you liked in this one, too!

The Editor.

⚡

Nick Kismet writes:

I was pleased to discover that the pulp genre is still alive, if very inconspicuous.

I can't seem to find any information about submission of new content. Is *Adventure Tales* open to new fiction from unpublished talent (and I use that term loosely) or is it mostly a venue for reprinted classics?

Unfortunately, ADVENTURE TALES is going to be mostly reprints. The one fictional exception may be a novel by Mike Resnick, which we are talking about serializing. It's the fourth of his Lucifer Jones books . . . which falls smack dab in the middle of what we're trying to do with AT.

The Editor.

⚡

W.M. Mott writes:

Recently I was contacted by a guy representing a web-based magazine called "Adventure Fiction."

He solicited stories and artwork, and an interview, then disappeared. Even his web site vanished.

Has anyone here heard of this "web magazine"? Was it perhaps in conflict with your *Adventure Tales* magazine?

Any info would be appreciated.

I have never heard of this web zine, and I can assure you that its disappearance had nothing to do with ADVENTURE TALES. *We encourage all new publications dealing with adventure fiction, pulp fiction . . . or come to think of it, fiction of any kind!*

Any reader with information about this lost publication should feel free to post a note to W.M. Mott about it on the ADVENTURE TALES *message board at:*

www.wildsidepress.com

The Editor.

www.ingramcontent.com/pod-product-compliance
Lightning Source LLC
Chambersburg PA
CBHW082016170626

46817CB00009B/3120